P9-EDE-381

Chryssanti had never forgiven Dimitri

Nor had she ever managed to forget him, despite her best efforts. Now his dark eyes took in her tall curvaceous loveliness. "You haven't wasted much time. My brother is a married man now, Chryssanti."

"So everyone keeps telling me!" she snapped.

As Dimitri's hand caught her outflung arm, an unfamiliar tingling sensation spread along her nerves. "You were a nice child, Chryssanti, if a trifle misguided. I hope maturity has not changed you."

"The years certainly haven't changed you, Dimitri Mavroleon!" she retorted. "You're still as arrogant and interfering."

As she made to pass, he blocked her path, his broad-shouldered figure oddly menacing. "Remember this, Chryssanti, I intend to personally make sure that you are never alone with Christos."

ANNABEL MURRAY has pursued many hobbies. She helped found an arts group in Liverpool, England, where she lives with her husband and two daughters. She loves drama: she appeared in many stage productions and went on to write an award-winning historical play. She uses all her experiences—holidays being no exception—to flesh out her characters' backgrounds and create believable settings for her romance novels.

Books by Annabel Murray

Don't miss any of our special offers. Write to us at the following address for information on our newest releases.

Harlequin Reader Service
901 Fuhrmann Blvd., P.O. Box 1397, Buffalo, NY 14240
Canadian address: P.O. Box 603,
Fort Erie, Ont. L2A 5X3

ANNABEL MURRAY

island turmoil

Harlequin Books

TORONTO • NEW YORK • LONDON
AMSTERDAM • PARIS • SYDNEY • HAMBURG
STOCKHOLM • ATHENS • TOKYO • MILAN

For: Tom especially.
And for all the other members of my family
and friends too numerous to mention.

Harlequin Presents first edition July 1990
ISBN 0-373-11283-1

Original hardcover edition published in 1989
by Mills & Boon Limited

Copyright © 1989 by Annabel Murray. All rights reserved.
Except for use in any review, the reproduction or utilization
of this work in whole or in part in any form by any electronic,
mechanical or other means, now known or hereafter invented,
including xerography, photocopying and recording,
or in any information storage or retrieval system, is forbidden without
the permission of the publisher, Harlequin Enterprises Limited,
225 Duncan Mill Road, Don Mills, Ontario, Canada M3B 3K9.

All the characters in this book have no existence outside the
imagination of the author and have no relation whatsoever to
anyone bearing the same name or names. They are not even
distantly inspired by any individual known or unknown to the
author, and all incidents are pure invention.

® are Trademarks registered in the United States Patent and
Trademark Office and in other countries.

Printed in U.S.A.

CHAPTER ONE

'ANOTHER letter from Greece, Chrys, darling?' Emily Forster's expression was troubled as she eyed her granddaughter's red-gold head bent so attentively over the sheets of thin blue paper.

Chryssanti recognised the source of the anxiety in her grandmother's voice. Some four years ago Chryssanti Forster—Chrys, as she preferred to be called—had paid her first visit to her late mother's homeland. And ever since then Emily had been afraid of losing her only granddaughter to the lure of Greece.

'Yes, it's from Lena Mavroleon. She's had her baby, a boy. She's calling him Nikki. She wants me to go to the christening. She wants me to be one of the godparents.'

'Shall you go?' There was still tension in Emily Forster's tone.

'I'd like to see Lena again,' Chryssanti said slowly, 'and I'd like to see the baby. Then there's Stephen, of course. I haven't seen him for years. He'll be nine now.'

'I wish your mother hadn't insisted on sending you and your brother to her people. Your grandfather and I would willingly have looked after you both.' Then, bitterly, 'It's not as if Stephen is a Mavroleon. He's a *Forster*, the only son of *our* only son.'

'Never mind, Gran,' Chryssanti consoled her, 'he'll be allowed to come and see you when he's older. And *I* came back, didn't I? *I've* no intention of toeing the Mavroleon family line. Grandfather Thalassios is a real

7

old tyrant—not like my lovely Gramps Forster.' Her
tawny eyes twinkled fondly as she glanced at the old man
whom she adored.

'I've often wondered though why you *did* come back
so suddenly,' Ned Forster said. 'At first your letters were
full of enthusiasm about Greece and your Greek
relations.'

'First impressions aren't always the right ones,'
Chryssanti said as she folded her letter. Not wanting to
be quizzed further on that particular subject, she stood
up and began to clear the breakfast-table. 'And if I
hadn't come back I wouldn't have had the chance to go
to university.' The previous summer she Had completed
her three-year B.A. Honours in the History of Art and
English Literature.

She moved quickly back and forth between breakfast-
room and kitchen, a tall, leggy young woman, yet, despite her height, inordinately graceful.

'So what will you do about Lena's invitation?' Emily
persisted.

'Em!' her husband chided. 'You can't keep Chrys tied
to your apron-strings for ever. She'll want to get married
some day, and then what? Of course she must keep in
touch with her mother's family.'

'I don't think you need worry about me getting
married for a long, long time,' Chryssanti told them.
'But I agree with Gramps—I think I ought to go. Not
just because it's family. Lena was very good to Stephen
and me.'

Lena Mavroleon, then Lena Thomas, had escorted the
eighteen-year-old Chryssanti and her small brother to
Greece. Lena had been especially kind and understanding during a particularly traumatic period of the

younger girl's visit. But this was an episode Chryssanti hadn't mentioned to her grandparents.

'You won't let *them* take *you* over body and soul?' Emily begged. By 'them' she meant the vast ramifications of the Mavroleon family, ruled by the autocratic, patriarchal figure of Thalassios Mavroleon. 'I know they've got a lot to offer, with their wealth and their islands.'

'Money isn't everything,' Ned Forster put in. 'Chrys has her head well screwed on. And don't forget, she'll be a rich young woman in her own right some day.'

'As for the islands,' Chryssanti said scornfully, 'they're nothing but a few lumps of rock sticking up out of the sea.'

But once the islands had meant rather more to her than that. The islands—and Christos.

It was raining as Chryssanti boarded the plane for Athens, raining and cold.

Typical English June weather, she thought with a shiver. But the little frisson of sensation was not wholly due to the climate. She was on her way now and there was no turning back. She'd been apprehensive too on that first visit to Greece. Then her mother, Irini, had been ill and about to have a serious operation. Chryssanti hadn't wanted to leave her. Nor had she any desire to meet her Greek grandfather. The wealthy shipping magnate had disowned his daughter many years before, when—against his wishes—Irini had married an Englishman, Stephen Forster.

But Chryssanti's apprehension had begun to fade from the moment she met Christos Mavroleon, her cousin. Christos had treated her as the adult she was fast becoming.

At the thought of Christos, her heart began to beat a little faster. She would be bound to see him. Any family celebration would bring the Mavroleons out in force, a daunting assembly. Yes, he would be at the christening. She wondered if he had changed at all. He would certainly see a vast difference in her. She was taller now, five feet eight in her stockinged feet, and her figure had matured to a ripe loveliness that widened and held male eyes. The full-lipped mouth, almost sulky in the child, gave the woman a promise of sensuality.

The sun was glaring down on the Bay of Athens as the aeroplane began its descent. And beyond were the first of many islands, a green and brown patchwork quilt, set in a deep blue sea.

With a barely perceptible sensation of impact the aeroplane touched down on the tarmac. The tension of landing over, there was an outburst of relieved chatter. Chryssanti had not been nervous. Long ago she had adopted the philosophy that if something was meant to happen it *would* happen. She reached for her hand-luggage and followed the stream of passengers out into the clear, blue, breathless atmosphere of a Greek summer's day.

She'd expected to have to take a taxi from the airport, but beyond the barrier she saw a familiar face.

'Lena! Oh, it's lovely to see you again. How are you?' But she didn't really need to ask. It was only too obvious that marriage and motherhood suited Lena Mavroleon, and Chryssanti felt an unexpected twinge of envy.

'Chrys!' Lena hugged her, then stood on tiptoe to kiss her cheek. 'You were lovely at eighteen, but you're positively beautiful now. How many hearts have you broken?'

Chryssanti smiled a little lop-sidedly. There had been boyfriends, of course, during her university days. But somehow none of them had managed to erase the image of a dark, handsome Greek. Her current escort, Terry, had perhaps come closest to doing so. He was a thoroughly nice young man, kind and fun-loving. He would make an eminently suitable husband and Chryssanti knew he wanted to marry her. Perhaps some day she would say yes. The outcome might prove more successful, she thought wryly, than leaving the choice to Cupid and chance.

Fortunately Lena didn't wait for an answer but swept her towards a waiting limousine.

'Home, Spyros, please.' Marriage to a wealthy man had given her a glossy veneer of sophistication. She was immaculately and expensively dressed. The once unruly honey-blonde hair was now worn in a neat chignon. But she was still the same Lena. She turned to Chryssanti with all her old impulsive curiosity as they settled themselves in the luxurious interior. 'Now, tell me all your news.'

'There isn't much to tell,' Chryssanti protested. 'I've told you most of it in my letters.'

'You haven't mentioned Domenicos lately.' Lena had once been personal assistant to Domenicos Theodopoulos, Chryssanti's great-uncle. 'You used to mention him quite regularly. You haven't fallen out with him, have you?'

'After all he's done for me? Goodness, no. He's a darling.' Domenicos had supported her during her years at university. 'It's just that...' She hesitated. 'This is rather embarrassing. Not the sort of thing you like to talk about, really. It sounds like bragging. He's made me his heir.'

'What about Petros?'

Chryssanti looked doubtfully at Lena, who had once been engaged to Domenicos's great-nephew.

'He and his wife were killed in an air-crash last year, in Texas.'

'I'm sorry to hear that, of course,' Lena said formally, 'Even though Petros played a dirty trick that nearly split Marcos and me up, I wouldn't have wished that on him.' Then, in a more relaxed manner, 'But it's a marvellous break for you, Chrys. You'll never have to worry about money for the rest of your life. What about Stephen, though?'

'Uncle Domenicos says Stephen doesn't need his money, not with the Mavroleon millions behind him. I suppose,' wistfully, 'Stephen is very Greek now?'

'Yes. He speaks the language as though he'd been born here. But he's happy, and Thalassios dotes on him.'

There was a short silence, during which both girls knew what the other was thinking. The powerful limousine ate up the miles of coastal road. On one side lay the brilliant Aegean, turquoise and transparent in the shallows, dark and mysterious in its depths. On the other side were rolling hills, covered in olive trees, grapevines and orchards.

Chryssanti couldn't hold back the question any longer. Anyway, Lena was waiting for it. She swallowed convulsively, then asked, 'How's Christos?'

'He's married now, as you know,' Lena's blue eyes were grave. 'His wife's expecting a baby and she hasn't been very well during her pregnancy. Chrys...?'

'Oh, it's all right, Lena. Heavens!' she attempted a light laugh. 'It's years since I saw him, and I was only an impressionable kid then. I'm quite over him by now.'

'I do hope so,' Lena told her. 'I wouldn't like...' she paused, 'anyone to be hurt.'

'What's his wife like?'

'She's a pretty little thing, dark-haired, inclined to be plump. Very shy. You'll meet her tomorrow night at our house. I'm giving a dinner party to welcome you back to Greece—just family, of course. You...you won't mind having to meet Christos?'

'Of course not. But when do I see the new arrival, my godson Nikki?' Deliberately Chryssanti changed the subject. 'And when's the christening?'

At the mention of her baby son, Lena's anxious expression changed to one of maternal fondness.

'You shall see him the minute we get home. The christening's not for a day or two. My husband...' At the mention of Marcos, she blushed prettily. 'My husband can't get away until then.'

'You're as much in love with him as ever, aren't you?' Chryssanti teased.

'More,' Lena said simply.

'You said Marcos can't get away? Does that mean the christening...?'

'Will be on Skiapelos, yes.' She grimaced comically. 'Yet another Mavroleon tradition!' But it was obvious she had no objection.

Chryssanti had never visited Marcos Mavroleon's town house in the modern part of Athens, and she looked about her with interest as she followed Lena up the front steps and into the wide marble-floored hallway. A semi-circular staircase hugged one wall which was hung with glowing oil paintings. Chryssanti would have liked to examine these more closely, but Lena swept her straight up to the nursery floor where a pleasant-faced nursemaid showed no objection to this disruption of routine.

'He's gorgeous,' Chryssanti murmured softly as she hung over the dainty crib. The baby had his father's olive-toned skin and dark eyes. 'And I should think his hair will be black, too. He's a pocket edition of Marcos.' And of Christos, too, she thought, for the cousins were very alike. This was how *his* child would look.

As if she knew what the younger girl was thinking, Lena put a hand on Chryssanti's arm.

'You'll have children of your own some day,' she said gently. 'Tell me,' she went on as they left the nursery, 'what do you plan to do now you've got your degree?'

'I haven't really decided. A postgraduate study maybe, or research. I thought I might eventually look for a job with an art publisher—as a researcher.'

'Surely you don't need a job as such?'

'Of course I do! I can't live on my expectations. For one thing, it would be ghoulish. But it's a matter of self-respect, too, and motivation. I wouldn't be happy as a drone. Surely *you* can understand that? You had a career.'

'Yes,' Lena admitted. Then, with a blush, 'But I've discovered I'd sooner be married. Have you kept up your painting?' she went on. 'I believe you used to be rather good.'

'Yes, I still paint. As a matter of fact, I brought some materials with me. I never go anywhere without them, just in case. But I don't suppose there'll be much opportunity to...'

'We'll *make* opportunities,' Lena told her. 'You don't have to rush back to England after the christening, do you?'

'No, but...'

'We're going to stay on Skiapelos for a bit. Marcos is taking some time off. He's supervising some building work on one of the other islands—the island he inherited from his father. We're going to have our own summer retreat there. You could stay on, too. Oh, please do,' she urged as Chryssanti looked doubtful. 'You'd be company for me while Marcos is busy.'

'I'll think about it,' was all a cautious Chryssanti would promise.

It was absurd to be so nervous, Chryssanti told herself as she dressed for dinner that evening. She was no longer a naïve teenager, uncertain of her place in this world of rich Greek shipowners. She was an intelligent, well-educated woman with a promising future ahead of her, no matter which field of her art she decided to pursue.

She need not feel self-conscious about her appearance, either. Entirely without false modesty, Chryssanti knew that she was extremely attractive. She'd seen the confirmation of that in enough men's eyes. And now the mirror in the luxuriously appointed guest-room told her the same story.

She'd chosen to wear white tonight, the lines of the draped bodice and flowing skirt inspired by classical Greek statues. The colour set off her vibrant red-gold hair, drawn back in a Grecian knot, and the fluid movement of the material did more than hint at the generously curved body beneath.

She leaned a little closer to the mirror as she outlined her wide, generous-lipped mouth with burnt orange, pausing for a moment to deplore the sprinkling of freckles on nose and cheeks which she considered marred her creamy complexion.

She was ready too soon. But she felt far too restless to stay in her room until the dinner gong sounded. From her window she had glimpsed a small but attractive garden, and if her geography was correct it could be reached via the large drawing-room. She gained her objective without encountering anyone, and imperceptibly her taut nerves relaxed. For it was a beautiful evening, still and balmy. The air was scented with basil and other aromatic herbs, mingled with pine and myrtle from the nearby hills. The moon was edging its way up over the rooftops, lemon yellow, then silver against the inky sky. It illuminated the garden as efficiently as any floodlight.

The garden had been designed to make the most of its limited space. Flagged pathways meandered through luxuriant shrubs and opened out into a square paved area where a demure stone nymph endlessly emptied an urn into an oval pool. A seat had been placed in just the right position to enjoy the sound and sight of the running water.

She would be glad when this first evening was over, Chryssanti thought as she sat down. Her first encounter with Christos was bound to be the worst. She didn't believe he'd ever guessed how she felt about him. He'd been kindly indulgent to his young English cousin. Perhaps he *had* flirted with her a little. But it had only been to put her at ease, Chryssanti recognised that now. To the immature girl she'd been then, it had seemed he returned her feelings.

She had no fear of betraying her emotions to him. She was mature enough now to be able to dissemble. Besides, she was well aware of the futility of harbouring any hopes where he was concerned. He was married, and Chryssanti had been brought up in a strict moral code. You didn't get involved with married men.

A footstep ringing on the paved area made her turn her head, and for a moment she fancied her thoughts must have conjured him up. She hadn't planned to meet him like this—alone. Feeling at a disadvantage seated, she stood up. Her eyes were almost on a level with his.

'Christos!' She was glad to note that her voice was steady, striking just the right note of friendly greeting. But panic had set up a fluttering in her pulses.

'Chryssanti?' For a moment he sounded doubtful. Then, 'It is!' He came closer. 'I hardly recognised you. You were little more than a freckled schoolgirl when I last saw you. What have you done to yourself?' His admiring gaze was on the statuesque picture she made. 'You have grown into an incredibly lovely woman.'

He was the same Christos she'd fallen in love with, her uncritical eyes told her.

'I've still got the freckles.' Chryssanti tried to defuse the tension of the moment. But the remark was a mistake, for he leant closer still to test the truth of her statement.

'Hmm, too many to count! But they suit you.'

'What's this, Christos? An assignation?' A curt voice made them both start—as though they were guilty of some misdemeanour, Chryssanti thought indignantly.

As she moved out of Christos's shadow, the moonlight identified her to the man standing a few feet away.

'Theos mou!' Dimitri Mavroleon exclaimed. 'You! I might have known!' Then, to his younger brother, 'Fortula was looking for you. You'd better go and see what she wants.'

Christos lingered only a moment. He had always deferred to his elder brother, Chryssanti recalled with some irritation.

'See you at dinner, Chryssanti.' Then, with a murmured apology, he was gone.

Chryssanti was left to face another man she had never quite managed to forget, despite all her best efforts. Nor had she ever forgiven Dimitri Mavroleon.

He moved towards her, his dark eyes taking in her tall, curvaceous loveliness. His tone was condemnatory.

'You have not wasted much time. How long have you been here? An hour or two? My brother is a married man now, Chryssanti.'

'So everyone keeps telling me!' she snapped. She'd been aggrieved to find that even Lena thought her capable of acting indiscreetly where Christos was concerned. Whereas nothing could be further from her intentions.

'Stay away from Christos!' Dimitri warned. 'His wife is not finding life easy at the moment. But she is a good wife to him and will be a good mother to his sons.'

His erroneous assumption about her goaded Chryssanti into anger.

'Of course, it wouldn't occur to you arrogant Greeks that she might have daughters? Women are second-class citizens as far as you're concerned, aren't they? Just breeding machines. Oh!' She spread her arms in a gesture of angry frustration.

'Stop behaving like a shrew. It does not become you.' Dimitri's hand caught her outflung arm, and an unfamiliar tingling sensation spread along her nerves. She gave a startled gasp and tried to pull free of him. But he tightened his grasp. 'You were a nice child, Chryssanti, if a trifle misguided. I hope maturity has not changed you.'

'The years certainly haven't changed *you*, Dimitri Mavroleon!' she retorted. Her husky, attractive voice became even more low-keyed in anger. 'You're still as arrogant and interfering. You still have a knack of showing up where you're not wanted.'

'And *you* wanted to be alone with Christos, as you did all those years ago?' He flung her arm from his as though it were a tainted thing. 'But of course, you were brought up in an immoral Western culture.'

She wasn't going to give him the satisfaction of an answer. In any case, if she denied it he wouldn't believe her. In the distance she heard the boom of the dinner gong. As she made to pass Dimitri, he placed himself in front of her, not touching her, but blocking her path. He was the tallest of the Mavroleons and his tall, broad-shouldered figure was oddly menacing, though she had never feared him before—only hated him.

'Remember this, Chryssanti. I intend to make it my personal responsibility to see that *you* are *never* alone with Christos.'

Just as he had four years ago, Chryssanti remembered as she stalked ahead of him, back to the house.

On her arrival in Greece she had spent a few days with Christos and Dimitri's mother, at her villa just outside Athens. She'd been shy and unhappy, worried about her own mother. Christos had taken her under his wing, done his best to win a smile from her. He had tried to take her mind off her troubles by thinking up interesting excursions, thus earning her devotion. But wherever they went they were always accompanied by his brothers, Manoli—and Dimitri. And it had been Dimitri who'd made a point of telling her, during her stay at her grandfather's home on Skiapelos, that Christos was engaged to be married.

She hadn't believed him at first. She had accused him of lying, of mischief-making. But even when she'd discovered the truth of his statement she'd still hated him for being the instrument of her disillusion, for witnessing her bitter unhappiness. That galled her most of all, that she'd let Dimitri Mavroleon see how much he'd hurt her. Well, he wouldn't get a chance to hurt her again.

Like everything else they did, the Mavroleons ate in style, Chryssanti thought, looking at the flowers, the white napery, the gleaming silver and crystal.

As Lena had promised, they were only a small family party—Anastasia Mavroleon and her three sons. Dimitri. Manoli, who was accompanied by his wife Marianthe. Christos and *his* wife, Fortula. As Chryssanti had noticed on her previous visit, men and women tended to gravitate to opposite ends of the room.

The meal had been prepared buffet-style. Lena announced that all was ready, but the men went on with their conversation as though they were deaf. Their talk, as usual, seemed to be of ships and shipping, though precedent was somewhat broken when Marcos asked after Dimitri's horses. Apparently he kept a string of racehorses at Newmarket.

The men continued to show no interest in the food and the women began to assemble plates of delicacies. But to Chryssanti's astonishment these were not for themselves. Instead they handed the loaded plates to their menfolk before attending to their own needs. Anastasia waited on Dimitri, and even Lena, Chryssanti noticed, conformed to this pattern of behaviour. She was unable to resist commenting.

Lena seemed quite unconcerned.

'Greek men expect their wives to put husbands and sons first. It is traditional.'

'It's ... it's *feudal*!' Chryssanti exclaimed. 'Marriage should be a partnership. Catch me waiting hand and foot on a man—like a servant!'

Though the men continued their self-imposed segregation, two of them at least were not wholly engrossed by the subject of business—Christos and Dimitri. Several times Chryssanti caught one or the other of them glancing her way. Feeling increasingly uncomfortable, she adjusted her seat so that her back was towards the group of men, and concentrated on the conversation she was having with Anastasia Mavroleon.

'It's lovely to see you again, Tassia,' she told the quiet, dark woman. 'I haven't forgotten how kind you were when I stayed with you.'

'You must pay us a visit while you're here,' Anastasia insisted. 'I was so sorry to hear of your mother's death.'

'Your letter was very much appreciated,' Chryssanti told her.

'Was *my* letter not appreciated?' A deep voice suddenly close at hand made her jump. 'You answered my mother's letter, as I remember. Mine you ignored.'

Inwardly Chryssanti knew she had been guilty of discourtesy, but at the time there had been no way she had wanted to communicate with Dimitri Mavroleon. She tilted her pointed chin at him.

'At a time like that, it's virtually impossible to reply to all the expressions of condolence. I felt my reply to your mother's letter covered *your* family.'

He was not deceived, of course. He *knew* why she hadn't answered. She saw his eyes glitter darkly, and then he was bent on revenge.

'The idea of having a buffet meal is so that one may circulate. You have been introduced to Fortula, of course. But you must get to know her better.' And

Chryssanti found a strong hand at her elbow, lifting her from her chair and propelling her across the room. Once again she was aware of a disturbing sensation that she put down to the annoyance she felt at his high-handed manner.

'I haven't noticed *you* doing much circulating,' she hissed at him. 'Or any of the men, come to that.' The rider was a mistake.

'Disappointed, Chryssanti? But then you would hardly expect Christos to dance attendance on you in front of his wife?' The cynical curl of his mouth was transformed miraculously into a pleasant smile as they reached Fortula's side.

'Chryssanti has met the other members of our family before. You two must get to know each other. I am sure you will find interests in common.' His dark eyes warned Chryssanti of the one common subject that was taboo. He went on smoothly, 'Fortula is a very accomplished watercolourist. You must get her to show you some of her work.'

Chryssanti sat down beside the other girl, her immediate interest not merely one of good manners, and soon the two of them were deep in discussion of techniques and subject matter. Pointedly she turned her shoulder on Dimitri, excluding him from their conversation. And after a while she felt him move away.

She knew what his ploy was, of course. She was to get to know Fortula and discover how eminently likeable she was, something she had soon realised without Dimitri's intervention. His idea obviously was that, liking Fortula, her feelings for Christos would be tempered by guilt.

As they talked, she had time to study Fortula. She was all that everyone had said of her. Quietly spoken, shy in her manner, she had a tendency towards plumpness which was of course exaggerated by her pregnancy. Though the discomfort she had suffered could not affect the olive of her complexion, her eyes were dark-ringed and there were lines of strain around her mouth.

'When is your baby due?' Chryssanti asked when the topic of art seemed exhausted.

'Not for another three months.' Wryly, 'And it seems like a lifetime already. Poor Christos!' Her eyes, soft and expressive of love, sought her husband. 'I am afraid I am a great trial to him.'

Following Fortula's gaze, Chryssanti reflected that Christos didn't seem to be suffering unduly. In fact, she noticed for the first time, he seemed to have put on weight himself, being no longer quite so slim and athletic-looking. His handsome face too bore traces of good living. But he was still Christos, she thought wistfully.

He must have felt the force of their combined gaze, for he turned and looked their way, then came towards them.

'How does it feel to be back in Greece, Chryssanti?' he asked.

'I'm not sure.' She smiled up at him. 'Ask me that again in a few days.'

He drew a chair to her side. Out of the corner of her eye Chryssanti became aware of Dimitri strolling, oh, so casually, towards them. He reached their little group just as Christos observed, 'I hope we shall see a lot of you while you are in Greece. You must dine with us one evening.'

'I thought you and Fortula were not entertaining at present,' Dimitri cut in. And to Fortula, 'You are looking weary, my dear. You must not overdo things.'

'I am rather tired,' she admitted with a glance half-pleading, half-apologetic, at her husband.

'For heaven's sake,' Christos said irritably, 'it's early yet. But if *you* want to leave, the chauffeur can take you home. I will get Manoli to drop me off later.'

'I doubt any of us will be staying much longer,' Dimitri put in quickly. 'Lena has only recently given birth, and I am sure Chryssanti must be tired after her journey.' His eyes dared her to deny it. He turned to his mother, chatting close at hand to Lena. 'It is time we were leaving.'

At once Anastasia concurred, giving proof once again—if it were needed, Chryssanti thought cynically—that in Greece a man's word was law, be he husband or son. It seemed women still lagged behind in equality. She caught Fortula's look of gratitude and was equally aware of Christos's pique at having his evening cut short so arbitrarily. He rose with a bad grace to assist his wife out of her chair.

'We must have a longer talk next time we meet, Chryssanti.' And she felt Dimitri's watchful eyes on her as she politely agreed. What did he expect, she thought angrily—that she should totally ignore Christos? Surely that kind of behaviour would be more open to misinterpretation than friendliness?

Her stay in Greece looked like being a minefield to be precariously negotiated.

The guests began to leave in a chorus of goodbyes. Anastasia repeated her invitation to Chryssanti.

'Come and stay for a few days. I am sure dear Helena will not mind sparing you to me.'

Chryssanti would have demurred, but Lena pressed her to accept.

'Of course you must go. I mustn't be greedy. But promise me you'll stay in Greece for a nice long time. You've no reason to rush home.'

'Then I'll send a car for you at ten o'clock the day after tomorrow,' Anastasia promised.

Though Dimitri was to all intents and purposes listening to something Marcos was saying, Chryssanti sensed that he'd heard this exchange. She wondered how he felt about her proposed visit and hoped he wouldn't be too much in evidence at the villa.

Now that Manoli and Christos were both married, Dimitri was the only one of Anastasia's sons still at home. Odd, that, since he was the eldest. Chryssanti wondered idly why he'd never married. Probably no one would have him, she reflected. But no, that wasn't fair. Just because *she* disliked him didn't mean he wasn't *some* woman's dream of perfection. He certainly wasn't lacking in physical attraction, she admitted reluctantly—if you liked that sort of thing.

His brothers, Christos and Manoli, were cast very much in the same mould as their cousin Marcos, with blunt, craggy features and full, rather sensual mouths. Dimitri's features were more sharply defined, with long, carved lips, his profile more that of a sculptor's concept of the Greek male. He was taller than any of his cousins. But his height had a matching breadth of shoulder and power of muscle.

Christos came towards her, hand outstretched, to make his farewells.

'I am glad you are going to visit Mother. It will be quite like old times to have you stay at the villa.'

'Except that she will see very little of *you*, Christos.' Dimitri's darkening glance made Chryssanti realise that Christos's clasp of her hand had gone on a little too long. Hastily she withdrew her fingers, only to find them encompassed instead by Dimitri's iron hand, exerting a warning pressure. His dark eyes held hers in an unfathomable gaze.

Unaccountably she was assailed by a sensation of alarm, the sudden, more rapid beat of her heart, which did not abate even when he released her. It was ridiculous to feel so...so *threatened*.

CHAPTER TWO

CHRYSSANTI looked forward to the visit to Anastasia's home with more apprehension than anticipation. She rather wished there had been some way she could have refused the invitation, but Greek people, she knew, took their hospitality very seriously.

'The car's outside,' Lena told her. 'On time, too. That's unusual for Tassia's chauffeur.'

Chryssanti gathered up her suitcase, handbag and her camera. She never went anywhere without the camera. There wasn't always time for sketching from life, and she didn't subscribe to the theory that it was cheating to paint from photographs.

'Enjoy yourself,' Lena adjured her.

'I'd rather be staying here,' Chryssanti confessed. 'Kiss Nikki goodbye for me.' Already she was enslaved by her friend's small son.

Accompanied by Lena, she went out into the hallway just as a maid opened the front door.

'Oh!' Lena exclaimed with pleasure. 'No wonder the car was on time.'

But Chryssanti stared with dismay at the tall figure of Dimitri Mavroleon dominating the threshold. So great was her dismay that she rushed into unwise, unpremeditated speech, felt Lena's surprise and saw the tightening of Dimitri's lips.

'Why have *you* come for me?'

In front of Lena he muttered some polite pleasantry. But when he had ushered her into the car and taken his seat beside her, he turned to her and demanded, 'Who were you expecting? Christos?'

Oh, he was hateful. 'Your mother's chauffeur, actually!'

'Then why was it I discovered my brother about to set out to fetch you?' he demanded as the limousine surged away from the kerbside.

'How should *I* know?' Chryssanti cried in exasperation. 'I didn't think Christos even lived with you now that he's married.'

'Normally he does not. But only yesterday he persuaded my mother that, since Fortula is having difficulties with her pregnancy, she needs the company of another woman. Her own mother died some time ago.'

Chryssanti's heart sank. These next few days were going to be even more difficult than she'd supposed. With Christos and Fortula under the same roof, she would be subjected continually to Dimitri's surveillance. It was time for plain speaking. She stared straight ahead through the windscreen, her hands clenched in her lap.

'Look, Dimitri,' her husky voice was earnest, 'we'd better get this straight. First, I was *not* expecting Christos to meet me, and second, I've no designs on him. I don't mess about with married men.'

His classical profile was stern and unrelenting when, unnerved by his implacable silence, she glanced at him.

'Did you hear what I said?' she demanded.

'Do you deny you have been in love with him since you were eighteen?'

'No, but I...'

'That is very flattering to a man's ego, especially that of a vain man. And Christos *is* vain.'

'But he doesn't know I...'

'A man whose wife is perhaps not as responsive to him because of ill health and fatigue.'

'I'm sorry Fortula's not well, but that's not *my* fault!'

'No, but if you were to take advantage of the situation...'

'But I shan't... Oh, you're impossible! I can't get through to you and I'm not even going to try. You're determined to believe the worst of me.'

She turned her head and studiously studied the passing landscape. They were traversing perhaps one of the most beautiful stretches of sea coast, a succession of bays with blue seas breaking on white-gold sands, and beyond was a high promontory crowned by white columns glittering in the sunlight.

'Look!' Chryssanti quite forgot she wasn't speaking to Dimitri. 'Oh, how beautiful! Please,' she turned imploring tawny eyes towards him, 'can we stop?'

Immaculately tailored shoulders shrugged.

'At Cape Sounion? Why not?' He turned the limousine off the road onto a twisting offshoot that ran out to the headland. As he braked to a halt Chryssanti snatched up her camera and scrambled out of the vehicle's air-conditioned comfort into the glaring sunshine.

'Where are you going?'

Reluctantly Chryssanti turned back.

'I *must* take some photographs,' she begged.

'With all the other trippers?' But even as he spoke he eased his long body out of the limousine.

'I don't mind them. And I might not get another opportunity.' As she started up the worn track that led to the promontory, he locked the car and followed her, his long strides easily bringing him level with her.

'Be careful. The surface is very uneven.' He put a hand beneath her elbow and she felt again the odd little frisson of sensation that she was beginning to associate with him. She wanted to shake off his touch and tell him she could manage. But she didn't want to antagonise him any more than she already had, and for the moment she needed his cooperation.

'Why are you so keen to take photographs of this place?' he asked as they ascended the hill. 'I had not rated you as an insatiable tourist.'

'I'm not. At least, the photos aren't just souvenirs. I'm hoping to do a series of paintings of Greece while I'm here—or at least gather the material.'

'I knew you had studied the history of art. I did not know you actually painted. Oils or watercolour?'

'Both. I usually sketch in watercolour, then work up the painting in oils later.'

'Just landscapes?'

'No, I do portraits too. I was hoping I might be able to persuade one or two members of the family to pose for me.'

'Which particular members?' The suspicion was back in his voice again, and she hastened to dispel the notion that she might be planning to ask Christos to sit for her.

'Your mother, perhaps? Thia Arietta? My grandfather, especially. An older face has so much more character.'

They had reached the summit now and Chryssanti paused to draw breath, not so much because of exertion but in appreciation of what she saw. Because of the clearness of the air, the radiance of the sun brought out the astonishing colours of the land and sea. From the temple she could see not only the bay and the mountains of Argolis, but also countless islands. The white Doric

columns she had glimpsed from the main road were
twelve in number, but there were gaps where others had
stood.

'I suppose it was a temple of some kind?' Greece, she
knew, abounded in temples.

'Yes, the temple of Poseidon. It was built to appease
the god of the sea when Athena was chosen instead of
him as the patron of Athens. In spite of this, mariners
were often shipwrecked on the rocks down there.' Dimitri
had not released his grip on her elbow and now he seemed
very close as he went on in his deep, melodic voice:

> '''Aloof they crown the foreland lone,
> From aloft they loftier rise
> Fair columns, in the aureola rolled
> From sunned Greek seas and skies.
> They wax, sublime to fancy's view
> A god-like group against the blue.'''

Somehow Chryssanti would never have suspected
Dimitri Mavroleon of having a poetic nature. He and
his family had always struck her, first and foremost, as
prosaic businessmen. But perhaps there *was* something
a little different about Dimitri. She looked at him with
a new curiosity.

'That was beautiful,' she told him ungrudgingly, her
eyes still on his dark, attractive face. 'Where does it come
from?'

'Lines by Herman Melville, inspired by this view.' And
as if he'd read her thoughts, he said, 'You are not the
only one who had a literary education.' His eyes met
hers and held them in a long, challenging look. They
were still standing very close together and suddenly
Chryssanti felt disconcerted by his proximity. Uncom-
fortably, she supposed it was possible to recognise a

man's incredible sensuality without liking him. With a little incoherent murmur she moved away and became very busy with her camera.

Obligingly Dimitri pointed out the hundreds of names that had been scratched by travellers on the temple's marble columns, among them that of Byron.

'So they had vandals even in those days,' Chryssanti commented.

'In Byron's time it wasn't considered to be vandalism. It was thought the highbrow thing to do.'

After a while she noticed him look at his watch and realised she was keeping him waiting. He probably had more important things to do than stand around on this hillside while she indulged her hobby.

'I'm sorry,' she apologised. 'I expect you want to get on.'

'For myself, I am not concerned,' he told her. 'But my mother will be anxious.'

'Don't you have to go into the office today?' she asked as they retraced their way to the limousine.

'No. I have decided to take some leave this week and next.'

'I suppose that means you'll be going to Skiapelos for the christening?' That had been almost a foregone conclusion, so she was not surprised when he inclined his dark head.

'It will be a very important family occasion, the first male of a new generation.'

It was not much further to the villa, high in the heat-shimmered, vine-covered hills bounded to the north by barren mountains, infertile but a true vision of classical beauty.

'It's just how I remember it,' Chryssanti exclaimed in delight as they drove between guardian cypresses and the building came in sight, huge and dazzlingly white, its architectural style reminiscent of the temple they had just visited. White marble steps led up into the reception hall, where Anastasia herself greeted Chryssanti with a kiss on both cheeks.

'We were beginning to think you were lost!' From behind Anastasia came Christos's drawl.

'I'm sorry about that,' Chryssanti told her aunt. 'It was my fault. I spotted this fantastic view and I simply had to take some photos. I'm hoping to take a lot while I'm in Greece.'

'I have given you the rooms you had before,' Anastasia explained as she led the way into an apartment whose windows gave views of the vine-clad hills beyond. 'I thought it would make you feel at home. Lunch is ready when you are.'

Again Chryssanti apologised for keeping her aunt waiting. Hastily she freshened up and hurried to join the others.

Fortula was not at lunch.

'She is having a tray in her room,' Anastasia explained. 'I worry about her. I shall be glad when the child is born. Now tell me, Chryssanti, is it true that Domenicos Theodopoulos has made you his heir?'

'I suppose Lena told you? Yes.'

'So you will be rich in your own right some day,' Christos commented. 'A splendid dowry for some fortunate man. Not that you *need* a dowry, with your looks.'

Chryssanti flushed—not at the compliment, she was accustomed to receiving those, but at the knowledge of Dimitri's disapproving stare.

'You will have to be careful that you do not attract fortune-hunters,' Anastasia said. 'I believe you are not engaged as yet?'

Chryssanti saw a chance to divert Dimitri's suspicions from her and perhaps also Christos's attentions.

'Not engaged, but there is someone who wants to marry me.'

'My dear, you must let your family meet him before you make any decision.'

Chryssanti was under no illusions. She knew Anastasia meant her *Greek* family.

'My grandparents like him very much,' she said firmly. 'And I think I'm quite capable of making up my own mind. Besides, I was going out with Terry before Uncle Domenicos remade his will.'

'But he must have known you had expectations? Your English grandparents are not poor. And he would have known of the Mavroleon connection.'

Chryssanti was beginning to feel a little harassed by this pressure, and wished she had never mentioned Terry's name. She sought to change the subject.

'Are there any other antique sites around here worth seeing?'

'I could take you to Mount Hymettus,' Christos said. 'You've heard of it?'

'Yes, I...'

'I have placed *myself* at Chryssanti's disposal for these next few days,' Dimitri intervened quellingly. Then, 'As Christos, says, there is Hymettus. There is also plenty to see in Athens itself.'

'I can explore Athens when I'm back at Lena's house,' Chryssanti said hastily. 'You're on holiday. You won't want to be dragged back into the city.'

'As I said,' he reminded her, 'I am at your disposal.'

Dimitri was going to unusual lengths to ensure she and Christos were never alone, Chryssanti thought later, during the siesta period. As she mulled over his persistent supervision, a theory began to form.

Dimitri's main concern obviously was for his sister-in-law. There was no doubt he was fond of her. Suppose there were something more? Perhaps he was in love with Fortula himself—which made his efforts on her behalf decidedly quixotic, since Fortula so obviously adored her husband. That could also be the reason why Dimitri had never married.

Somehow Chryssanti found she didn't like the idea of Dimitri being in love with his sister-in-law. *Her* anxiety was on Christos's behalf, she supposed. She wouldn't want him to be made unhappy. And yet she felt she knew Dimitri well enough now to know that his principles would never let him break up his brother's marriage. So why this feeling of uneasiness? she wondered as she drifted into sleep.

She was unused to sleeping in the daytime, and the siesta left her feeling unrefreshed and dull. What she needed, she decided, was a swim. Anastasia's villa, being out of town, boasted a much larger garden than Marcos's house, and its grounds contained a large kidney-shaped pool.

She donned a bikini in a jewel-shade of emerald and, pulling a towelling robe about her, she made her way through the villa and out on to the patio surrounding the pool. Dropping her robe on the tiles, she dived cleanly into the sparkling water.

Chryssanti had a strong overarm style, and she swam several brisk lengths of the pool before turning on to her back and floating on its limpid surface.

A hearty burst of applause startled her upright to see Christos crouching on the edge of the tiled surround.

He too was dressed for swimming, in brief black trunks that left very little to the imagination.

'You still swim like a dolphin,' he said as he slipped into the water and waded towards her. 'Do you remember me telling you that?'

She did, of course. Over the years she had treasured every remark Christos had ever made to her. But now she was a little uncomfortable at the obvious admiration in his dark eyes. She glanced around, but they were alone.

'H-how's Fortula feeling now?' she asked, and saw him grimace.

'I have never known a woman make such a business of carrying a baby,' he complained. '*Theos mou!* It's a natural enough thing.'

'Some women find it more difficult than others,' Chryssanti told him. 'She's not very tall...'

'Not like you!' Again his eyes held an unmistakable message. 'I doubt if *you* will have much trouble when your turn comes.' His gaze appraised her generous curves and, embarrassingly, his hands traced their shape in the air. 'You have child-bearing hips.'

'Christos,' she began protestingly, 'I...'

'Marcos was fortunate,' he went on. 'He managed to marry a woman of his own choice. My wife was chosen for me when we were both children.'

'I believe those sort of marriages often work quite well,' Chryssanti said. She was becoming increasingly uncomfortable at the trend the conversation was taking. She began to wade towards the edge of the pool. 'I sometimes think everyone would do better to have their partners chosen for them, or at least to choose them scientifically, instead of relying on luck.'

'It is not so much fun,' Christos said. He had followed her, and in trying to increase her pace Chryssanti slipped.

He was not slow to take his opportunity, and she surfaced to find herself in Christos's arms, held rather too close against his water-slicked body.

All too conscious of the touch of his skin on hers, Chryssanti found herself unable to speak as her eyes roved over the familiar good looks which had haunted her dreams for so long.

'You're beautiful!' There was a note of awe, of wonder, in his huskily spoken words. 'Chryssanti, you don't know how I wish...' His words were cut short by a splash close at hand as another body dived into the pool and surfaced nearby.

It was Dimitri. Who else? Chryssanti thought fatalistically as cold, inimical eyes met hers.

'I...I slipped.' She was annoyed to find herself actually explaining her situation.

'And Christos was at hand to rescue you? How convenient!' His voice was harsh.

'Are you trying to imply something?' Christos flared up immediately. He scowled at his brother, eyes flashing, hands clenched into fists at his sides.

'If the cap fits, little brother!'

Chryssanti had seen Christos angry before and knew that, like many Greeks, he had a quick, volatile temper, prone to intensity and histrionics, which only made Dimitri's behaviour more of a contrast. *His* anger showed itself in a brooding silence, a withdrawal into a shell of displeasure. He demonstrated that now by ignoring his brother's belligerent stance.

'If you are here to swim,' he told Chryssanti curtly, 'let us swim.'

'Thanks,' she told him, 'but I've been in a long time. I'm going to get dressed.'

'A few more minutes will not do you any harm, and I wish to talk to you.' His eyes were stony.

Inwardly Chryssanti groaned. More lectures, no doubt. But Christos was scrambling out of the pool, and if she left now it would only feed Dimitri's suspicions. Tired by her earlier exertions, she did little more than dog-paddle and watch Dimitri's energetic lapping of the pool.

He swam well, his strong arms and shoulders cleaving the water like some relentless machine.

At last he stopped, surfacing close to Chryssanti.

'Finished?' she enquired with sweet sarcasm.

'Think yourself lucky I decided to swim first and talk second.' And, as she raised haughty, enquiring eyebrows, 'I could not trust myself to speak to you straight away.' There was quiet contempt in his face. 'Just why *did* you decide to come back to Greece, Chryssanti?'

She looked at him in surprise.

'Several reasons. Mainly Nikki's christening, of course. And I would like to see my brother. Then it's a marvellous opportunity to study Greek art and get some material for my paintings.'

'Yes, yes,' irritably, 'those are the ostensible reasons. But there was more to it than that. You came back to see Christos, *ne*?'

'Oh, Dimitri, for heaven's sake!' Chryssanti said exasperatedly. 'I thought we'd been through all that. If that was my reason, why have I waited four years?'

'Maybe you have heard that all is not well with his marriage?'

'How would I have heard that?'

'You and Lena write to each other regularly.'

'Lena has never once mentioned anything like that.' Chryssanti was indignant on her friend's behalf. 'To suggest that she'd indulge in that sort of gossip is an insult to Lena.'

'All right.' He spread his hands in reluctant apology. 'I too would not have thought it of Lena. But maybe Christos wrote to you himself.'

'Well, he didn't, and I don't have to stand here and listen to these insulting insinuations.' She turned to go, but his hand shot out and restrained her. His grip was hard but his voice was surprisingly gentle, almost pleading.

'Chryssanti, you could bring more sorrow on yourself in the end than you bring on anyone else. I do not want to see you hurt.'

'You weren't worried about that four years ago,' she snapped, and his expression hardened once more. 'Anyway, you needn't concern yourself on my account.'

'Then if you will not take heed for yourself, think of Fortula. She is a nice girl. I am warning you, Chryssanti, do not start something you cannot finish, or *I* will have to deal with you.'

'And what precisely does that mean?'

'Stay away from Christos and you will not need to know. Now, get dressed and fetch your camera. We are going out.'

'I don't want to go anywhere with *you*,' she retorted. 'And with the opinion you seem to have of me, I shouldn't think *you* want *my* company.'

'You are a guest in our house, to be looked after and entertained. My mother is occupied with Fortula. If you wish me to believe you are anxious to see something of Greece—rather than my brother—I suggest you take advantage of my offer.'

Chryssanti was seething as she showered and rubbed herself dry. It was nothing short of blackmail. 'Do as I say or else.' Or else what? Odd, she brooded, that she should find Dimitri so intimidating. It was only the fact that she didn't quite know what lay behind his threat that was making her comply with his peremptory orders.

If they were going sightseeing as Dimitri had intimated, she had better dress suitably. She pulled on yellow cotton slacks, a matching T-shirt and low-heeled slip-on shoes.

As she approached him she was aware of his dark eyes sketching a swift sexual assessment of the way her slacks hugged her hips, the way the T-shirt clung lovingly to her generously curved breasts.

'Good,' he said approvingly. 'I had not expected you to be ready so quickly.'

He was probably accustomed to women spending a lot of time glamourising themselves to go out with him, Chryssanti reflected as he steered her towards the waiting limousine. She wondered where he was taking her, but she wasn't going to give him the satisfaction of asking. But she was not left long in doubt.

'I thought, since Mount Hymettus was mentioned and it is near at hand, we would go there. Does that meet with your approval?'

Chryssanti shrugged.

'You're in charge, apparently.'

'True!' He seemed unperturbed by her sarcastic reply.

As Dimitri had said, it was not far to Mount Hymettus, whose golden-brown slopes formed one of the ring of mountains sheltering Athens. It was possible, he told Chryssanti, to drive to the summit. The view was well worth while.

'But perhaps you would care to walk? It will give you more opportunity for photography?'

Chryssanti agreed and set off eagerly up the steep pathway which ascended the bare slopes covered with scented flowers, buzzing with industrious bees. These flowers, Dimitri explained as he kept pace with her, produced very good honey.

'You have heard of the honey of Hymettus?'

She nodded. It was world-famous.

Their climb brought them eventually to a deserted Byzantine monastery of mellow red brick surrounded by dark cypresses, its roof and small dome covered with dark pantiles. And here Chryssanti found plenty of work for her camera. Around the monastery was a small garden, and she was attracted by the sound of a stream nearby that filled the air with bubbling melody. Tracing the sound to its source, she found that the spring issued from the head of a stone ram.

There were a few other people about. But on a Sunday, Dimitri said, the winding road up the mountain would be alive with Athenian families, coming to the spring to picnic in the shade of the giant old cypresses and plane trees and to take home the water.

'The spring is mentioned in our legends as a source of fertility,' he told her. 'Young men and women who wish to have children come here and take home containers filled with what they believe to be magic water.'

'Do you believe in that sort of thing?' Chryssanti asked curiously.

He smiled wryly. 'I have not yet had occasion to doubt my fertility.' And, for no particular reason that she could think of, Chryssanti flushed scarlet.

Dimitri had not exaggerated about the view from the summit. The prospect included many inland regions as well as the cluster of the Cyclades grouped round the central islet of Delos and, nearer at hand, Cape Sounion and Athens.

'Thank you for bringing me here,' Chryssanti said as they made their way back to the limousine.

He inclined his dark head.

'It was my pleasure.'

Chryssanti doubted it. He probably regarded it as more of a duty, not only as her host but as part of his self-imposed task to keep her and Christos apart.

As they drove away Chryssanti looked back at the mountain. The sun was just setting and Hymettus was engulfed in an unbelievable flush of deep violet.

'It's incredibly beautiful,' she sighed.

'So is much of Greece,' Dimitri told her. 'But for me the most beautiful are the islands of Skiapelos. Do you remember much of the islands?'

'Not a lot,' she confessed. 'I was only there about a week, and I wasn't as interested in scenery in those days.' It was an unfortunate remark, capable of misinterpretation.

'No, you were not!' His deep, rich voice was suddenly harsh, and she guessed he was remembering that on Skiapelos she had been obsessed only with Christos. He proved her right by saying abruptly, 'In those days you were too much in love with Christos. Chryssanti, *are* you still in love with him?' As he glanced sideways at her a faint wince of pain crossed her features.

'Four years is a long time,' she said evasively.

'Some things remain the same, no matter how much time goes by.' He drove in silence for a while. Then, 'Even if Christos had been free to marry you, you would never have been happy with him. He is not man enough for you.'

'You don't have to denigrate him to me, in addition to everything else you've done,' she told him with low-key fury. She wished he would leave the subject alone. He was like a dog worrying a bone. 'Apart from anything else, it's disloyal. He's your *brother* for heaven's sake.'

'Which is why I do not wish to have to punch him on the nose. And if I see him hanging around you again, making a play for you, that is exactly what I shall do.'

'Christos is *not* making a play for me, any more than I'm making a play for him. What you saw today...'

'Perhaps I see more than you do, Chryssanti. I see a man who is going through a period of dissatisfaction with his marriage—a period which will pass if it is allowed to do so. And I see a very attractive woman who has carried a torch for him for years. It is a dangerous combination.'

Chryssanti was becoming extremely irritated by his harping on this same subject. By his very persistence he was creating a situation that did not actually exist. Whatever her feelings for Christos, there was no way she planned to break up his marriage.

'Just what *is* your concern in this?' she demanded. 'Apart from being a general busybody? It seems to me that you have an almost unhealthy interest in the state of Christos's marriage. I suppose it couldn't be that you're hoping it *will* break up? You don't by any chance fancy Fortula for yourself?'

The limousine swerved into the side of the road as he braked and turned towards her, his face contorted by anger, and in fascinated apprehension she watched the vein at his temple that throbbed distendedly.

'Do not dare to make such an accusation to me.'

'Why not? What's sauce for the goose is sauce for the gander, Dimitri. You sling mud at me and I'll sling it right back. Ever since I arrived in Greece you've been making insinuations about me and Christos, even though I've told you time and again I'm not here to make trouble. How about giving me the benefit of the doubt? You withdraw your accusations and I'll withdraw mine.'

He did not reply at once. Instead he sat staring into her tawny eyes, darkened and widened with anger. His gaze held hers for what seemed an interminable time. Then, incredibly, his stern features relaxed into a smile. It was a revelation to Chryssanti, a transformation, totally disarming, emphasising the dark attraction of his face.

She swallowed and lowered her lashes to obscure the sudden internal churning which she felt must be reflected in her expression.

'Very well, Chryssanti,' she heard him say, 'we will call a truce, *ne*?'

Her lowered eyes observed his hand thrust out towards her and, although oddly reluctant to do so, she put her slender fingers into his. His hand was warm and strong, and at the contact she felt every sinew of her body tighten. It was an unfamiliar sensation that first alarmed then, even more, strangely panicked and angered her. Hastily she withdrew her fingers from his clasp.

To hide the riot of emotions swirling within her, she kept her eyes averted and her voice cool.

'Truce,' she agreed. 'Hadn't we better get on? I don't want to keep Aunt Tassia waiting for a meal two days in succession.'

CHAPTER THREE

'WHAT are you two going to do today?'

Breakfast at Anastasia's villa was customarily eaten out of doors, on the patio by the swimming pool, and this morning was no exception.

Chryssanti wished her aunt wouldn't address her and Dimitri as if they were a couple, as if their plans for the day must automatically include each other.

'*I* thought of having a lazy day here by the pool,' she told Anastasia.

'There will be plenty of lazy days on Skiapelos when the weather will be hotter even than it is now. *Now* is the time to do your sightseeing.' Dimitri of course, laying down the law.

'Most of the things I want to see are in Athens,' she argued, meaning that she could well leave them until her return to Lena's home.

'Then I could give you a lift on my way to the office,' Christos said. He was dressed for business this morning in a dark-coloured but lightweight suit which made him the younger, slimmer Christos she remembered. 'No need to drag Dimitri away.'

Irresistibly Chryssanti's eyes were drawn to Dimitri, to observe his reaction to this suggestion. He was breakfasting in shorts and a short-sleeved sports shirt, the outfit revealing a great deal of his strong bronzed limbs, lightly coated with soft dark hair. Something about him stirred a deep, responsive shudder within her—dislike, of course.

He spoke to Christos, but his gaze locked with hers. 'Escorting Chryssanti is no penance to me. I shall be only too happy to do so. Sometimes I think, engrossed in work, we tend to forget the beauty of our own heritage. I shall enjoy seeing it through Chryssanti's eyes.' He rose with a murmured excuse to his mother. 'I will change into something more suitable for the city.'

Chryssanti watched as he strode away, supreme self-confidence expressed in every ripple of those broad, compactly muscled shoulders. He hadn't even waited to see if she'd make any protest.

'It is very good of Dimitri to give up his time like this,' Anastasia said, following her elder son's departure with a complacent smile. 'He is a very busy man. He cancelled many appointments to spend these few days at home.'

'Appointments which *I* have to keep instead,' Christos grumbled as he too rose from the breakfast table. 'I would not have objected to some time off.'

'You will have that time next week,' Anastasia reminded him, 'when we all go to Skiapelos for little Nikki's christening.' There was mild reproof in her tone, the nearest Chryssanti had ever heard her aunt come to criticising any of her sons. Sons, like husbands, were always right and to be deferred to. To Chryssanti, Anastasia explained, 'Only Manoli will remain in Athens next week. One director of the Mavroleon Corporation must be there to conduct business.'

'Where shall we begin?' Dimitri asked as they drove into Athens.

Chryssanti shrugged. She was still feeling a little piqued at having her time thus organised for her. She was feeling distinctly perturbed, too, to think that Dimitri had deliberately taken time off work to do so. Greek businessmen did not so lightly evade their responsibilities.

'Then may I suggest the Acropolis first, before the day becomes too hot?' It was phrased as a question but Chryssanti received the distinct impression that a decision had been made. 'It has become a tourist cliché, of course, but one can hardly say one has been to Athens and then confess one has not seen its most famous piece of architecture.'

'I've seen it from a distance.' The grey and red cliff of the Acropolis with its crown of broken marble temples was visible from almost any point in Athens.

'From a distance!' he said scornfully. 'As a student of art you must penetrate to its very heart. You must feel as well as see.'

Though she was unwilling to admit it, he was right, Chryssanti thought as they stood on the summit, two hundred feet above the surrounding plain, gazing up at the Parthenon, its honey-coloured columns of Pentelic marble rising from a massive limestone base. The structure did not possess a single straight line of any length. And just as worthy of admiration, if not as awe-inspiring, was the exquisite little temple of Athena Nike— the Giver of Victory—its narrow Ionic columns made even more delicate by the imposing Doric colonnade of the Propylaia.

Their approach, littered with slabs of marble, had been crowded with sightseers talking a dozen different languages, interspersed by garrulous guides. But none of it could detract from the awe she felt at this, her first prospect of the ruins.

From the summit it was possible to gain some idea of the size of Athens, overrunning its surrounding hills, its houses lapping the edge of the mountains.

'Do you know the story of the founding of Athens?' Dimitri asked, and as Chryssanti shook her head, 'It is said both Athene and Poseidon wished to become its patron, and Zeus decreed that the honour should go to whoever produced a gift which would prove the more useful to man. The Sea King struck the earth with his trident and out sprang a horse. But Athene produced an olive tree, and this symbol of peace and plenty was judged to be the more valuable.'

It helped to have a knowledgable companion, even if it had to be Dimitri. He knew his Greek mythology—and history, too, she admitted grudgingly. Which was not as inevitable as it might seem. Many people lived within yards of historical sites and thought no more of them than they did of more modern architecture, the convenient supermarket or multi-storey car park.

But Dimitri was not just a mine of factual information. As he had at Cape Sounion, he surprised her by the poetic turn of his mind.

'It is necessary to visit the Acropolis more than once. Its moods change with the time of day. In early morning its columns are as cool as your pearly skin.' His words, the glance of his dark, deep-set eyes, made Chryssanti flush self-consciously, but he went on, 'At noon they pulse and shimmer with the heat of the sun. At sunset they glow gold and red as if on fire, just like your hair. But at night, when there is a full moon, then it has a truly mystical beauty.'

Chryssanti mumbled something, she knew not what. She was used to receiving compliments, but she hadn't expected to receive them from Dimitri Mavroleon. It made her feel uncomfortable. It was as if a savage lion had suddenly become a purring hearthside cat.

The visit to the Acropolis had occupied the whole of the morning, and Dimitri suggested that they return to the villa in time for the siesta period.

'The afternoon will be too hot and you must be careful with your complexion not to become burned or overtired.'

But it was not Chryssanti's last visit to the city with Dimitri. He could be very pleasant company, she discovered with some surprise, his conversation searching and stimulating. Educated in England and Paris, he spoke several languages fluently. She learned a great deal about his own interests: his collection of art treasures, his racehorses, the real estate which he collected as avidly as his brothers and his cousin collected ships.

Probably that was why he'd never settled down, Chryssanti reflected, since it seemed his interests kept him on the move, gypsy-like, from country to country.

And yet he was a businessman, too. His chief function with the Mavroleon Corporation was the supervision of teams of experts who compiled data about oil refineries and generating stations. He was responsible for feasibility studies and financial calculations.

Like the rest of his family, he took his religion very seriously. Wherever he was on a Sunday morning, he attended the local Greek Orthodox church.

In the days that followed their visit to the Acropolis he uncomplainingly accompanied her around the museums. The National Archaeological with its comprehensive collection of ancient Greek art, the Byzantine with its superb collection of icons and the Benaki, displaying Greek national costumes, jewellery and handicrafts.

'This must be awfully boring for you,' she apologised.

'Not at all.' But his eyes were on her animated face rather than on the displays before them. 'I think I have enjoyed it as much as I hope you have done.'

And she *had* enjoyed herself, so much so that it came as quite a surprise to realise that her stay with Anastasia and her family was at an end and that she must return to Lena's house to prepare for the journey to Skiapelos.

'I am sorry I have not spent much time with you myself,' Anastasia apologised as she bade Chryssanti farewell. 'With Fortula here I have been more occupied than I expected. But I shall see more of you on Skiapelos. And I believe Dimitri has looked after you very well?'

He had, and it would have been churlish not to admit it. On the journey into Athens Chryssanti tried to express her thanks. Not usually at a loss for words, she found it difficult. Something about Dimitri affected her in a way she'd never experienced before. She did not wholly understand it, though she knew it had something to do with the sexual attraction he exuded, an attribute which made it impossible to be totally at ease with him.

'It has been my pleasure,' he said gravely when she stammered her thanks. 'And I think——' he shot her a swift sideways glance '—it has enabled us to reach a better understanding of each other. Perhaps now you do not view me quite so much as an ogre?'

There was no answer to that, since he still made her oddly nervous. And, new understanding or not, he had not ceased to keep a vigilant eye on her when Christos was around, so much so that she hardly dared speak to Christos or look at him. And Christos had noticed, she was sure of that.

'I will not come in,' Dimitri told her as the limousine stopped at Lena's front door and he took Chryssanti's hand in farewell. 'Lena will be busy with preparations for the voyage.' He paused. 'I look forward to seeing you again tomorrow.'

Did he really, she wondered as she mounted the front steps of the town house, her hand still tingling from his grasp, or was it just a polite platitude? She was glad to be back at Lena's, of course she was, but all the same there was a feeling, almost like regret, that the past few days were over. She tried to analyse it. Probably, she decided, it was due to seeing Christos again. Even though they could never be anything to each other, inevitably it must have aroused old nostalgic longings.

'Are you ready for the ordeal?' Lena asked Chryssanti next morning. She was laughing.

'Ordeal?'

'Being subjected to the scrutiny of all your relations. A lot of them will be making the trip with us, and they'll all be curious to see how and if you've changed in the past few years. Don't be surprised if you get asked a lot of questions, too. I've discovered that Greek people have a way of taking an avid interest in everyone's personal life, family or otherwise.'

Marcos Mavroleon's yacht, the *Poseidon*, was berthed at Piraeus, the ancient port of Athens. Despite its picturesque waterfront, Chryssanti found it too noisy a place for her liking. Passengers shoved their way on to the clamorous ferries, taking leave of their relatives and friends in tones that—if she had not known better—could have been taken for tremendous quarrels. There were bursts of laughter and raucous music from the many *tavernas* lining the waterfront. The yacht basin was crowded with boats ranging from eighteen-footers to millionaires' sea-going vessels.

Chryssanti was not as awed by the size and appointments of the *Poseidon* as she might have been, since she'd made her previous journey to Skiapelos on board her cousin's yacht. As on that occasion the vessel was swarming with Mavroleon relations, some of whom—like the nun Arietta—she already knew.

The young nursemaid had whisked baby Nikki below as soon as they came on board, and Lena was free to stroll the decks with Chryssanti, watching the preparations for departure.

'Tassia couldn't come after all,' she told Chryssanti as they leaned on the gleaming brass rail of the after-deck. 'At the last moment Fortula wasn't feeling at all well, so they're staying at the villa.'

'What about Christos?' Chryssanti asked involuntarily.

'Oh, *he's* here...'

'...which makes one wonder at his lack of concern for his wife, and his motive in making the trip,' another voice close at hand put in, and the two girls swung round to find Dimitri Mavroleon standing behind them. His dark eyes were on Chryssanti's face, which had flushed self-consciously.

'Tassia said Fortula urged him to come,' Lena said. 'She feels very guilty about the way her health is affecting his social life.'

'*Fortula* has nothing to reproach herself with,' Dimitri observed, still in the same harsh voice. His emphasis on the name made Chryssanti wonder just whom he *did* find worthy of censure. The relaxed, friendly man of the past few days was not in evidence. His sensually curved mouth was drawn into stern and forbidding lines.

'I must go below and see that Nikki is all right,' Lena decided. 'Dimitri,' she flashed the tall man a friendly smile, 'I'm sure you'll look after Chrys for me.' Without waiting for an answer, she hurried away.

'I don't *need* looking after, you know,' Chryssanti objected as Dimitri showed signs of fulfilling Lena's commission. 'In fact, I think I'll go below myself.' She made as if to do so.

'And miss our departure? I thought you would be busy with your photography. But perhaps you are not interested in seascapes?'

'Yes, I am.' Chryssanti's camera, as usual, was about her neck.

'Well, then!' He made an expansive gesture. And, as if that settled the point, he leaned against the railing, watching her expectantly.

Damn him. Why did he always have to be so right? Chryssanti wondered, as she took sightings and focused her camera. Of course she must not miss this perhaps never to be repeated opportunity. She concentrated not only on the coastline but on the activities of the crew as they weighed anchor and the great yacht set sail. The crystal haze-free light of Greece was ideal for photography, and she looked forward to some spectacular results.

There was an unmistakable dignity to this land, she thought as the coastline slid by, a majesty to the starkly brilliant landscape, the mountains around Athens standing in razor-sharp clarity against the sky. A dignity of character that was shared by the man silently watching her, Chryssanti realised. Not for Dimitri the emotional volatility of so many of his countrymen. Even when he was extremely angry, that anger was kept within bounds. She found herself wondering if he ever displayed any other emotions, wondered if he had ever been in love.

At thirty-one, he was only eight years younger than his cousin Marcos.

'What are you thinking?' he asked suddenly, catching her speculative gaze on him, and at once she averted her eyes.

'How incredibly blue the sky is,' she improvised hastily. 'If I paint it that way, no one will ever believe it.'

'Only those who have been to Greece,' Dimitri agreed. 'Cézanne said of our skies that they were not blue colour but blue light.'

This man was full of surprises, a veritable mine of general knowledge. Chryssanti was aware that, over the past few days, he had risen considerably in her estimation. It was a pity in a way, she thought wistfully, that he was still so mistrustful of her. She would rather have him for a friend than an enemy.

'Do you have enough material now?' his deep voice broke across her thoughts. 'It is time to be dressing for dinner.'

The Mavroleons dressed for dinner on board the yacht just as they would in the dining-rooms of their palatial villas. The men were distinguished in their conventional black with snowy white shirt-fronts, and there was a fortune in jewellery around the necks of the women.

Chryssanti had taken considerable pains over her own appearance, and she knew that the emerald green dress flattered her red-gold colouring. The halter neckline hinted at the generous curves of her breast and emphasised the grace of her creamy shoulders and the long swan-like neck. At the back a deep V plunged to her waist, making it impossible to wear a bra. She had chosen not to wear any jewellery, believing, correctly, that her own vibrant youth was adornment enough.

Marcos was at the head of the table, Lena at its foot, otherwise there was no formal arrangement. Chryssanti found herself seated next to an elderly uncle on one side and on the other side Christos, who had attained his objective so neatly that Dimitri could do nothing without causing comment.

Chryssanti felt subtly flattered that Christos had sought her company, but she was troubled too, guilty at her own pleasure and aware of Dimitri's disapproval. She almost wished Christos hadn't singled her out. But after all, she argued with herself, there was nothing wrong in Christos sitting next to her and talking to her. She was just a little afraid that her reactions to him might be difficult to cope with. Married and out of her reach he might be, but he was still the man to whom she'd been so strongly attracted four years ago, and she was only human.

'I've had no chance at all to speak to you,' Christos complained during the first course. 'Dimitri has completely monopolised you.'

'Well, you can talk to me now,' she pointed out.

'Dinner-table talk!' he scoffed. 'Small talk. Nothing of importance can be said with thirty pairs of ears listening.'

But then, Christos shouldn't have anything to say to her that others could not overhear. Chryssanti toyed nervously with the heavy silver cutlery.

'I'm sorry Fortula didn't feel well enough to make the trip,' she said.

'Oh!' Christos shrugged. 'She does not enjoy family gatherings anyway. But let us not talk of Fortula. Let us talk of you. Tell me all about yourself, what you have been doing since I saw you last. And how you have grown into such a beauty.'

For the next hour, as they consumed course after course washed down with sweet white wine, Christos questioned her closely, his head bent attentively to catch her answers above the general hubbub of conversation, It gave them an air of intimacy, and Chryssanti dared not look in Dimitri's direction. She wished Christos would pay a little attention to his other neighbour, conscious that she should make an attempt to converse with the elderly uncle on her left.

'When you were at the villa you spoke of a man,' Christos probed, 'who wants to marry you. Tell me about him.'

'I'm sure you can't be interested in Terry,' she protested.

'I am interested in everything that concerns you.'

It was said with such intensity, so much *double entendre* in the words, that it seemed a wise precaution to enlarge on what she'd told Anastasia about Terry, exaggerating his importance in her life a little.

'This man is not for you,' Christos told her. 'You should have married a Greek. Especially since you are half-Greek yourself. You will not be happy married to a milk-and-water Englishman.' He leaned a little closer, and there was a more urgent note in his voice, a glint in his dark eyes. 'You would find that we Greeks have real warm blood in our veins.' He'd had constant recourse to the wine throughout the meal, and Chryssanti suspected he was more than a little drunk. 'The man who marries you, Chryssanti,' he went on fervently, 'will be very fortunate. *Very* fortunate.' He rested his hand on hers, and when she would have withdrawn it he increased his pressure.

It was ironic that Christos should be attracted to her too late, and Chryssanti felt that perhaps things were getting a little out of hand. Involuntarily, for the first time during the meal, her eyes flickered towards Dimitri. As she had suspected, he had not missed his brother's increasing intimacy of manner, nor the hand resting on hers. Venom hardened his eyes and his handsome face was a cold mask.

What was he thinking? It seemed to matter, though for the life of her she couldn't think why. His opinion shouldn't matter to her one way or the other.

Just at that moment Lena gave the signal for the ladies to leave the table. Chryssanti had never imagined a day when she would be relieved to escape Christos's company. It was Dimitri's fault, of course, she thought as she rose, succeeding at the same time in withdrawing her hand. Dimitri was making far too much of these little incidents and making her unnecessarily self-conscious. OK, perhaps Christos *was* a bit of a flirt, but she couldn't believe he would really be unfaithful to his marriage vows. And that was what Dimitri's watch-fulness implied.

'See you soon, Chryssanti,' Christos said quite au-dibly. 'I shall not sit long over the port. There are better ways of spending an hour or two.'

In the nearby salon the women fell into the easy con-versation of long acquaintance. Lena, as the hostess, was much in demand, and Chryssanti felt a little like a spec-tator on the sidelines. She felt uneasy for another reason. If, when the men left the dining-table, Christos *did* make a beeline for her, Dimitri would not be far behind. He couldn't make a public scene, of course, but she didn't doubt his ability to create an unpleasantly tense atmo-sphere. It would be better if she retired before the men rejoined the ladies.

On this decision she slipped unobtrusively away, intending to make for her cabin.

'Chryssanti! Where are you going?' Christos was just leaving the dining-room as she emerged from the salon.

She started as guiltily as if he had been Dimitri.

'I...I'm rather tired. I thought I'd have an early night.'

'Tired!' he scoffed. The Greeks seemed indefatigable, keeping unusually late hours. Probably the custom of the afternoon siesta gave them their unflagging energy. 'It is just the close atmosphere down here. What you need is some fresh air and exercise. Come!' And before she could protest he grasped her elbow and steered her aloft.

The *Poseidon* rode at anchor, and it was dark now except for a fugitive moon and the yacht's rigging lights. The foredeck was deserted. The crew would be eating, too. All was silent except for the gentle lapping of water against the side of the boat.

'At last,' Christos sighed. 'I thought I was never to have you to myself.' In a shadowy corner of the deck he slipped an arm about her waist.

Chryssanti swallowed nervously and tried to free herself.

'Christos, I don't think you...that is...we...'

'What is wrong?' His grasp tightened. 'Do you not like me any more?'

'It's not that. I...'

'Four years ago, as I remember, you were very fond of me. Very fond!' She hadn't realised he knew. He had both arms about her now and he was too close. She could smell the wine on the warm breath that brushed her averted cheek. 'Do you deny it?' he demanded.

'No, but...'

'Dimitri was always around then, curse him. But for a while we have given him the slip. Let us make the most of it.' His head came nearer, his mouth seeking hers.

'But you weren't interested in me in those days,' she protested a little breathlessly.

'Was I not?' he asked tenderly.

'No!' she insisted a little more firmly.

'What a blind young fool I must have been. But I am interested now, Chryssanti. Very, very interested.' Again he sought her mouth and again she managed to evade his seeking lips.

'But you *shouldn't* be!' she protested. 'You're married now.'

'How delightfully naïve you are.' He laughed softly. 'Marriage does not inhibit a man's ability to see, to think, to feel.'

'Perhaps not,' she retorted, 'but he ought to resist such feelings.'

He caught her still averted chin in one hand and turned her head to face him, just as the moon sailed out from behind concealing clouds, illuminating both their faces. He stared into her troubled eyes.

'Tell me, Chryssanti, when you heard, four years ago, that I was to be married, did that make any difference to your feelings for me?'

'N-no, but...'

'Have you thought about me at all during those four years?'

'Yes, but I...'

'And when you knew you were coming to Greece this time did you think about meeting me again?'

'Of course, but...'

'So my being married made no difference to your feelings for me? Then why should it make any difference to *my* feelings for *you*?'

'I just know that it should.' She managed to complete her sentence this time.

'Well, it doesn't.' It was an insidious whisper, and, with her chin still trapped in a painful grasp, this time she could not evade his mouth.

For a moment, in shocked surprise, she remained still under his almost violent onslaught. She had imagined so many times in the past what it would be like to be kissed by Christos. And this was the reality. And it shouldn't be happening.

Someone else thought so, too.

Before she could make any attempt to struggle free there came a violent intervention. Christos was dragged forcibly away from her. A tall, dark silhouette against the moonlight, Dimitri Mavroleon inserted himself between them. Instead of Christos's hot, wine-scented lips on hers there was the harsh grating of Dimitri's voice.

'*Epiph!* Christos, are you insane? For goodness' sake, man, you are married.'

'Damn you, Dimitri!' Christos reeled under the force of his brother's attack. Perhaps the wine had something to do with it too. 'Why are you always where you are not wanted?'

'It is just as well I am,' his brother retorted. Then, 'You have a wife, Christos,' he repeated.

'So? A man may marry more than once.' Christos sounded sulky now.

'What the hell are you trying to say?' Dimitri's voice had become dangerously quiet and some of his younger brother's bravado vanished.

'Nothing. Just making a statement of fact,' he muttered.

'You do not deserve a wife like Fortula,' Dimitri told him. His voice was edged with contempt, and again Chryssanti wondered at his energetic championship of Fortula. She found herself wondering if that was why Dimitri was so alert to her feelings for Christos, because of his own feelings for Fortula. 'You had better go below and sober up,' Dimitri told his brother. 'And in future, stay away from Chryssanti.'

For a moment Chryssanti thought Christos would defy him, but then he shrugged and turned away. Leaving her alone to face the music, she reflected apprehensively.

'And *now*,' Dimitri said, 'I'll deal with *you*. I warned you, Chryssanti.' His hand shot out and grasped her chin, pulling her towards him. His touch was like a brand, sending shivers of some nameless emotion through her. She blinked nervously.

'Let go of me!' she demanded. But his fingers only tightened more inexorably.

'Oh, no!' He growled the words. 'Not before I tell you exactly what I think of little tramps who play around with married men.'

At the opprobrious term, she gasped indignantly.

'I told you before, *I don't*.'

'No?' He jerked her closer. 'Then what would you call that display over dinner, this assignation on deck?'

'It wasn't—isn't—like that,' she protested. 'I couldn't help Christos sitting next to me at dinner. And...'

'You did not seem to find his company distasteful. Your heads were continually together.'

'I was just being polite.'

'I noticed your manners did not extend to making conversation with your other neighbour.'

'No...I...there wasn't much chance.'

'Exactly.' It was said on a note of triumph.

'And I didn't arrange to meet Christos on deck,' she rushed on before he could say anything else. 'It...it just happened.'

'There are ways of *making* things happen,' he sneered. 'I thought you had a boyfriend at home, Chryssanti. What would *he* think of your behaviour, I wonder?' His continued grasp of her chin was painful and Chryssanti felt the first stirrings of anger.

'Who appointed you my keeper, or the arbiter of Christos's morals?'

'So!' It was a hiss of sound. 'You admit your behaviour smacks of immorality.'

'I admit nothing!' Seen in the fitful moonlight, her delicately chiselled nostrils flared her anger. 'In any case, I don't have to account to you for my actions.'

'Perhaps you would prefer to account to Fortula?' His words sobered her a little. As Dimitri had predicted, she'd liked Christos's wife.

'No, I...'

'I thought not. It is one thing to try and steal another woman's husband, another to face her with your guilt.'

'I am *not* guilty. Will you stop interrupting? Just shut up and listen for a moment. I haven't said anything about stealing her husband. Nor do I intend to. It was Christos who...'

'...hinted at divorce?' He ignored her injunction about interrupting. '*Would* you marry a divorced man?'

'I've no religious scruples about it, if that's what you mean.'

'No scruples at all, if you ask me.'

'Well, I *didn't* ask you.' Chryssanti was really angry now. And angry she was like a beautiful roused tigress with her red-gold hair and blazing tawny eyes. 'I wouldn't have thought it would bother *you*. Didn't I read somewhere that a Greek—even a religious-minded one—can marry three times?'

He released her chin, but only to clamp his hands on her shoulders, administering an ungentle shake that made her richly coloured hair tumble about her face.

'So you have ambitions to be Christos's second wife. You little...'

'No!' she protested. 'I didn't say that!' She realised with dismay that her anger had taken her on to dangerous ground. What was all this about, anyway? she wondered wearily. She had no intention of breaking up Christos's marriage, so why go on with this defiance of Dimitri?

'Christos is a fool, of course,' Dimitri said. 'But I cannot blame him for wanting what seems to be on offer.' His voice had taken on a different note now, yet she sensed that it was equally dangerous. 'And I must admit, too, that you have a lot to offer,' he went on softly, narrowing the gap between them until his face was only inches from hers.

Nameless terror made her shudder. Then he spanned those last few inches, her soft body pressed to his hard one in an iron clasp, his mouth taking hers in a bruising punishment, and though she resisted with all her strength he pressurised her lips, forcing them to part and give him access to their delicate inner surface.

As his tongue invaded her mouth, quite unexpectedly strange sensations rippled through her, a weird mixture of anger and fascination, and she made a little sound in her throat of mingled protest and unwilling pleasure.

His kiss deepened, his lips softening. His lips became coaxing, passionate, and Chryssanti felt liquid fire streak along her nerves. Against her will she found herself responding to his kiss, and she felt the answering hammer of his heart against her breasts. His hands moved from her shoulders to her smooth, cool back, down the exposed flesh to her waistline. But, as his fingers slipped beneath the silky material and worked their way round to her unprotected breasts, alarm restored her slipping sanity.

Somewhere she found the strength to bring up her hands against his chest, deeply aware as she did so of the muscular hardness of flesh and sinew. Somehow she forced him away from her, found breath to speak.

'What do you think *that's* going to achieve?' she demanded shakily from the safety of two or three feet away.

'That was a warning,' Dimitri's voice was husky, 'a foretaste of what you can expect if you go on with your pursuit of my brother.' Then, his voice strengthening, 'If you must have a man while your boyfriend is out of reach, why not settle for me? I have no ties, no wife to be hurt.'

'*You?*' She was in control again now, and she injected all the scorn she could muster into the word. 'What would I want with you? What would any woman want with you? Nothing, obviously,' she taunted, 'since you're still single.' Then, as he made a move towards her that promised retribution, cravenly she turned and fled.

To her relief he did not follow her. For if he'd chosen to do so she would have stood no chance against his superior length of stride. But this time she gained her cabin unchallenged.

As she removed her make-up she stared in the mirror at her bruised mouth. The scene on deck confirmed what she had already suspected, that Dimitri Mavroleon was a dangerous man to cross. Oh, how she hated him. She wished she need never see him again. She was glad to think she'd dismissed his preposterous suggestion with so much derision.

But as she lay awake she found it less simple to dismiss Dimitri himself from her thoughts, or to shake off the memory of his kiss, the touch of his hands on her bare flesh.

She was ashamed of that momentary pang of pleasure she'd felt. But Dimitri couldn't take any credit for that, she assured herself. It was Christos she'd been thinking of when Dimitri had made love to her. It was strange, though, that she couldn't remember how Christos's kiss had felt, apart from the memory of a rather stale taste of wine. Not exactly a romantic recollection. And she didn't recall smelling alcohol on Dimitri's breath. His had been warm, natural, untainted. His kiss had excited her. Was it possible to learn about physical passion from a man you hated?

Chryssanti shivered. She *was* still in love with Christos, wasn't she? Any other interpretation of this comparison was unthinkable. Even though he was unattainable, she'd always loved Christos. He'd filled her thoughts for so long that to stop loving him would leave her with just an aching void.

CHAPTER FOUR

'Are you all right, Chrys?' Lena asked when they met at breakfast next morning. 'You look tired. Didn't you sleep well?'

'Not very,' Chryssanti admitted.

'Why was that, do you think? Bed not comfortable?'

It was the last thing she'd felt like doing when she got up, but Chryssanti had to laugh.

'The bed was the last word in comfort. I can't imagine Marcos owning anything that wasn't the best of its kind.'

'You were warm enough? Too warm?' Lena persisted with a hostess's anxiety.

'Nothing like that,' Chryssanti hastened to assure her. 'Just ... just things on my mind.'

'Forgive me if I seem to be prying,' Lena said hesitantly, 'but is it anything to do with Christos? You seemed to be enjoying his company last night. I was hoping, after all this time, you'd be able to meet him without too much pain. Perhaps I was wrong?'

'It has caused a few awkward moments,' Chryssanti admitted. 'But nothing I can't handle, Lena, honestly. It's ... it's just *Dimitri*!'

'Dimitri?' Lena sounded surprised. 'What's *he* done to upset you? Apart from Marcos, of course, I always think Dimitri's the nicest, the kindest of the Mavroleon men.'

Chryssanti was about to launch into a description of Dimitri's hostility, his suspicious attitude whenever she and Christos came into contact. But they were no longer alone. Various members of the family party, Dimitri and Christos among them, were drifting into breakfast, and the conversation, perforce, had to become general.

Chryssanti was disconcerted when, having selected his breakfast from a side table, Dimitri came to sit beside her. It was to prevent Christos doing so, of course. His proximity caused peculiar tremors in her insides—embarrassment, no doubt—and no wonder after last night. She concentrated fiercely on what Marcos was saying.

'We'll be making a stop at Mykonos later today, to pick up Marianthe and her parents.' Though Manoli and his wife had a villa on the outskirts of Athens, Marianthe had taken the opportunity of the family expedition to Skiapelos to go on ahead and pay a visit to her old home. 'If anyone wants to go ashore,' Marcos continued, 'we will be there for a few hours.'

'Mykonos is well worth a visit,' Dimitri observed, and with everyone listening Chryssanti could hardly ignore the fact that his remark was addressed to her.

'I know. I've been there,' she said shortly.

Lena had caught the little interchange.

'You didn't see much of it though, Chrys,' she protested. 'Only the harbour and the Lychnoses' home. You should get Dimitri to take you to see the view over the town. I'm sure he wouldn't mind?' She looked at Dimitri for confirmation.

'And if Dimitri is too busy, there is always Christos,' an elderly aunt put in with blithe ignorance of any undercurrents. 'He's the only other one young enough to make the climb.'

'I am *not* too busy,' Dimitri said curtly. 'I shall be pleased to oblige you, Lena, as always.'

Chryssanti hadn't thought for one moment that he'd want to oblige *her*, but her answer was tart.

'Everyone seems to assume I *want* to go ashore. Actually, I've got some letters to write.'

'You'll have lots of time to do that before we anchor,' Lena told her. 'Then you can post them on Mykonos.' To Chryssanti, under cover of the general conversation, she whispered, 'It will give you and Dimitri a chance to make up your differences.'

Again Chryssanti couldn't enlighten her, and it would have seemed a little too pointed and unnecessarily churlish to make any further excuses. And later that day, after the siesta, in sight of the thatched sentinel windmills of Mykonos, she reluctantly prepared to go ashore.

The shops on the quayside looked interesting, but Dimitri seemed in no mood to pause and Chryssanti wouldn't ask him. Beyond the harbour, narrow cobbled streets climbed the hill, twisting and turning and leading off one another in a fascinating maze.

'This island is very popular with tourists,' Dimitri told her as they walked up from the busy quayside and through the whitewashed alleys, flanked by icing-sugar houses. 'Not only for its own sake, but as a jumping-off place for Delos, the sacred island.'

Chryssanti made no reply. She had determined to remain aloof. But she was interested in spite of herself as he went on, 'Delos is sacred to Apollo and to Artemis, who were said to have been born there. The island is deserted now, apart from the sheep. You must go there some day. The terrace of lionesses there could have been sculpted by a modern artist. Have you ever thought of trying your hand at sculpture?'

'No,' Chryssanti shook her head. But she thought that if she had, Dimitri would have made a fine model with his striking, clean-cut features. The thought came in spite of herself. After his behaviour last night she was reluctant to find anything admirable about him.

'You are very monosyllabic today,' Dimitri said.

'Are you surprised, after last night?' she retorted sharply. 'Your company *was* rather thrust upon me.'

'Naturally, you would rather I was Christos!' He could be as abrasive as she.

'There's no "naturally" about it!' She was stung into lengthier speech, her tawny eyes blazing. 'If I've told you once, I've told you half a dozen times, I'm not "after" Christos. You must be the most stubborn, obtuse man I've ever met. *Why* won't you believe me?'

'Because the evidence is all to the contrary.'

'*Circumstantial* evidence. Just because you've found me twice with Christos in misleading circumstances...'

'You do not deny you were kissing each other last night?'

They had reached the bare, sun-drenched hill high above the town. Below them was the deep blue taffeta of the sea, the attractive port and innumerable little churches, their cupolas in a variety of delicate pastel shades. The air was redolent with the scent of sage and thyme. Chryssanti threw herself down on the dry, colourless grass.

'*He* was kissing *me*. There *is* a difference.'

She hadn't imagined Dìmitri would risk his immaculately creased trousers on the ground, but he lowered himself to sit beside her. He lay back, linking his hands behind his head, a picture of relaxation, she thought resentfully. While she was as taut as a bowstring.

'You would have me believe you were not returning his kisses?' A pregnant pause, then, 'You returned *mine*.'

Chryssanti's face was already flushed with heat and the exertion of the climb. Even so, her colour deepened as she remembered that kiss and her unexpected reaction to it.

'O-only for a moment. You...you took me by surprise.'

'What was the surprise, Chryssanti?' he asked softly. 'That you could enjoy another man's kiss as much as you enjoyed Christos's? For you *were* enjoying it.'

Somehow she had to quash his arrogant certainty.

'OK.' She shrugged. 'So I enjoy being kissed. It's a pleasant activity. It's meant to be. You surely don't imagine you and Christos are the only men who've kissed me?'

'No,' he said slowly, 'I did not imagine that.' He sounded vaguely displeased. 'And have you always enjoyed *every* man's kiss?'

'Some more than others,' she fenced.

'And where do we rate on your scale of pleasure, Christos and I, against your boyfriend Terry?'

'Oh, for heaven's sake!' Chryssanti bounced to her feet again. 'This is a ridiculous conversation. We're not talking about a talent show. What do you want?' she demanded as he stood up, his superior height looming over her. 'Marks out of ten?' The ridiculousness of the situation suddenly overcame her indignant embarrassment and she began to laugh, a full-throated, attractive chuckle. Amusement lit her tawny eyes. Solemnfaced, she was beautiful. Laughter brought that beauty to startling, vibrant life.

'You should laugh more often,' Dimitri observed.

She sobered as quickly as her mirth had exploded.

'I do, when the occasion and the company warrant it. I don't usually find *you* amusing.'

'No,' he agreed. 'Nor do you find me likeable. Is that not so?'

Chryssanti hesitated, remembering times in the past few days when, enjoying his company, she *had* come close to liking this man. She didn't exactly dislike him. And yet sometimes she felt she *hated* him—an odd inconsistency. She wasn't usually emotionally inconsistent. But she'd hesitated too long over her reply.

'No need to answer,' Dimitri said harshly. 'Your silence speaks for itself. Come. We had better make our way back to the yacht.'

It was beginning to grow dusk as they descended the hill in silence, a silence that Chryssanti found oddly depressing. And though she cast around in her mind for some remark to break it, a non-controversial topic, nothing came to mind.

It was Dimitri who finally spoke. He halted in his stride and looked down at her. He still sounded angry.

'Perhaps we could at least reach an agreement to be civil to each other, for the sake of family harmony at this time.'

'I've never been rude to you in front of anyone else,' she protested.

'No.' His voice was more even as he made the concession.

'I wouldn't be rude to you in private if…if you stopped accusing me of things I haven't done.'

He considered this for a moment, running a hand through the coarse, springy black mane of his hair. Then, 'Very well. In future I shall try to give you the benefit of the doubt.'

'Thanks!' she said sarcastically.

'But a truce is a two-way thing. Can you bring yourself to try and be friends with me, Chryssanti?'

'You make it very difficult for anyone to be your friend.'

'Not if I want their friendship.'

Why would he want *her* friendship? Again she hesitated.

'Would it help if I apologised for my behaviour last night?'

Hands in pockets, red-gold head on one side, she considered his grave features. 'That would rather depend on whether it was just expediency or whether you meant it.'

'I mean it,' he told her, 'and if I am to take your word for things, then you must take mine.' He held out his hand. 'Friends?'

'Friends,' she agreed, but she kept her hands thrust firmly into the pockets of her jeans. She hadn't forgotten the last time they'd shaken hands.

He didn't seem put out by her avoidance of physical contact. Instead he smiled, the smile that she had only seen once before for her, and which so transformed his face.

'This calls for a celebration.' He tucked his hand through the crook of her arm and steered her back into the maze of streets, some of them two-donkeys-narrow, to a small *taverna*.

'I don't drink,' she protested. 'At least, not very often.'

'A little wine will not harm you,' he coaxed. 'And you do eat?'

This was undeniable.

'But won't we be expected back on board?'

'Marcos will not sail until after dinner, and no one will be concerned if we eat ashore.'

The *taverna*, an ordinary enough whitewashed building on the outside, had more charm within. Gaily coloured cloths covered the tables. The walls were covered with cane-work decoration, folk-art and plaster grottoes.

Hollow gourds, corn-cobs and strings of garlic hung from the ceiling. The kitchen was part of the public domain, with all the food—cooked or waiting to be cooked—on display. It seemed to be the practice for customers to order after a personal inspection rather than from a menu.

Dimitri ordered a *moussaka*—a sort of shepherd's pie, but made with slices of aubergine between the layers of mince. On top, instead of potato, there was a thick crust of eggs and toasted cheese. Chryssanti found the accompanying wine a little harsh at first, but as Dimitri refilled her glass she became accustomed to the taste.

A Greek *taverna*, Chryssanti soon discovered, was an individualistic mixture of a restaurant, bar and palace of varieties. Pulsating folk music accompanied the meal, interspersed by the occasional song from one of the diners. Greeks, apparently, took a great pride in their singing and never, Dimitri assured Chryssanti gravely, did they sing badly. One singer, a man in his fifties, with a moustache and thinning grey hair, seemed especially popular, being called upon time and again for a rendering. The patrons seemed to spend hours over their meals.

'Don't they have any homes to go to?' she asked Dimitri wonderingly.

He smiled.

'You will find that we Greeks like to be surrounded by our friends, by music and laughter. We shun quiet and solitude. Except perhaps,' he became thoughtful, 'when we are alone with one special person.' And Chryssanti found herself wondering if he had a particular person in mind. If he had been anyone else, she might have asked him. But there was something about Dimitri that made her uneasy of intruding on his thoughts, of seeking any intimacy.

The middle-aged man was singing again, eyes closed, his head tilted back, his throat strained in the difficult voice control the song demanded. He had a splendid bass voice and the applause was becoming even more enthusiastic, the patrons rowdier in a mounting *kephi*—good spirits.

'Opa! Opa!' they cried. *'Opa! Opa! Huh!'* Glasses of wine pounded the tables.

'Watch!' Dimitri adjured Chryssanti. He hitched his chair close to hers and she was aware again of the stunning aura of maleness that was his. 'Soon you will see something which, strictly speaking, is forbidden. But a favourite singer or dancer can make his audience forget rules and regulations. And this man is both.'

Sure enough the man had begun to dance, arms outstretched, fingers clicking like castanets. It resembled the proud measure of a toreador before the threatening horns and eyes of a bull. The dancer moved with a power that held all eyes, every step a mastery of grace.

As he danced the noise from the audience grew in volume. And when the volume of cheers and shouts could grow no louder came the climax.

'Now you will see it,' Dimitri breathed in Chryssanti's ear. *'Spasimo!'*

He didn't interpret the word, but it wasn't necessary as first one plate then another smashed loudly on the stone floor. The patrons were on their feet, smacking their hands in time to the music, pausing in the wild rhythm only to snatch up another plate and crash it to the floor.

Chryssanti found herself clapping as energetically as anyone, and as Dimitri stood, she stood too. Plates were smashing all around the agile feet of the dancer. Dimitri handed Chryssanti a plate and she stared at him doubtfully.

'Go on!' he urged. 'Throw it! Do not worry. The *taverna* keeper will be reimbursed for the damages.'

She threw it and found herself laughing, cheering. She was part of this lively scene. It was part of her heritage. Smiling, she looked up into Dimitri's face and saw his eyes, dark and liquid with some unfathomable emotion.

At last the noise and the smashing of crockery subsided and order began to be restored. But Chryssanti was still possessed by a nameless euphoria. Someone had placed two more glasses of wine on their table. The bottle she and Dimitri had consumed seemed not to have done her any harm. Recklessly she swallowed the contents of hers.

Dimitri put his arm about her waist and steered her to a corner of the hot, smoky room where a flight of steps led upwards. She didn't know where they were going, but she let him propel her ahead of him until they came on to the flat roof of the *taverna*.

'So we can watch the sunset,' Dimitri explained.

The sun was already very low on the horizon, flushing the sea with mother-of-pearl; the sky was striped green, pink and smoke grey. As they watched, the sun slipped out of sight and a silvery moon rose tranquilly in the opposite quarter, sky and sea mingling together in a universal softness. The pageantry was over.

Chryssanti drew in a long, rapturous breath. She was feeling quite light-hearted—and a little light-headed, she realised. Dimitri's arm was still about her waist. Her senses absorbed the warmth of him and she leaned on him a little, suddenly in need of support.

'Chryssanti?' His voice was questioning and she looked up at him, her tawny eyes still dazed with the splendour of the sunset. She was in a state of heightened awareness of everything. She smiled beatifically at him. His clasp tightened suddenly and a contraction, pleasurable but oddly painful, moved inside her as Dimitri bent his head closer.

'Th-thank you for a lovely time,' she said. It seemed necessary to articulate very carefully. And her careful enunciation was marred by a very decided hiccup. She was surprised when Dimitri began to laugh. It was a rich, whole-hearted sound. She'd never heard him laugh that way before.

'Chryssanti, I do believe you are drunk!'

Unoffended, she considered the idea gravely.

'If I am,' she said with a little gurgle of laughter, 'it's your fault. I told you I wasn't used to drinking.'

'Oh, Chryssanti!' He breathed her name on a gentle note and pulled her into his arms. 'You should get drunk more often.'

Her face was innocently turned up to his, her soft lips without defence, his for the taking.

As his mouth touched hers, her heart gave a great lurch within her. The unique scent of his skin, compounded of aftershave and masculine odours, seemed to envelop her in its aura. It was a long, tender kiss, but he made no attempt to touch her in any other way, and he withdrew before she was ready for him to do so. She made a little murmuring sound of protest.

'Time to go, Chryssanti,' he told her. His hand at her elbow, his touch impersonal now, he led her back through the still crowded *taverna* and into the dark streets.

There was silence again as they made their way back to the harbour, and as the exercise and the air began to clear her head Chryssanti's mood of euphoria faded. She felt stunned and nauseous, and she knew a sickening sense of shame. She had allowed the wine, the mood of the *taverna* and the sunset to go to her head. Up there on the flat roof she had practically offered herself to be kissed—by Dimitri, of all people. And after the fuss she'd made about him kissing her last night. No wonder he was quiet.

It was a relief, on the quayside, to join up with Marianthe and her parents, waiting for the launch to take them out to the *Poseidon*.

'Chryssanti!' After a curious glance at the still silent Dimitri, Marianthe greeted her warmly, though they had met only a few nights ago at Lena and Marcos's villa. 'But we didn't have much opportunity to chat then. And I haven't had a chance to tell you,' she added *sotto voce*, with a glance at her parents, 'everything that happened after I ran away that time.'

It had been intended that Marianthe should marry *Marcos* Mavroleon. The match had been made when she was literally in her cradle. But only weeks before the wedding, aided and abetted by Lena and Chryssanti, Marianthe had left Mykonos and gone into hiding with a former schoolfriend.

On board the yacht, the two girls, arms linked, wandered around the decks reliving that day and the subsequent events which had led to Marianthe's marriage to Manoli, the Mavroleon she really loved.

'I don't blame you a bit,' Chryssanti told her. 'I wouldn't let anyone else influence *my* choice of a husband. And,' she chuckled, 'you certainly did Lena a good turn.'

Marianthe grinned.

'Marcos marrying a foreigner certainly caused a family furore. It was an uncommon occurrence. Intermarriage between islanders is the norm—even more so among big shipowners, so that ships and shares stay in the family.'

'You'd think the Mavroleons would be rich enough in their own right.'

'Ah, yes, but in a large family, once the sons are old enough to join the business, the interests are separated and each man is supposed to branch out for himself. It's a continual process. Like the Hydra they grow more and more heads, which means launching more firms, buying more ships. When Grandfather Thalassios dies the bulk of *his* fortune will go to Marcos as the eldest grandson. The others will have to fend more or less for themselves. So you see, extra money is not to be sneezed at.'

'So was Grandfather Thalassios furious when Marcos married Lena?'

'At first. But he cooled down when he realised the Mavroleons would still be linked to my family. Christos did as he was told and married money. That only leaves Dimitri to settle down.'

'I suppose he'll be looking for a rich wife, too?'

'Probably. No, I should say definitely.'

'I'm surprised *he* wasn't betrothed from childhood.'

'He was engaged once. His fiancée died—about six or seven years ago.'

'Oh?' Chryssanti was intrigued. 'And has there never been anyone else?'

'A few women friends, naturally. He's very attractive to women. He has great *philotimo*. But there's been no one special, I think.'

Not for the first time, Chryssanti wished her mother had not refused to teach her children her own language.

'*Philotimo?*' she queried, and Marianthe wrinkled her brow.

'It's a difficult word to translate into English. It's a kind of aura—a combination of attributes—everything that is desirable in a man. Pride, self-respect, honesty. Oh, and so much more.'

'I think I understand,' Chryssanti said slowly.

Their perambulations had brought them to the pool deck, which they were surprised to find a hive of activity. The large, mosaic-tiled swimming pool had been covered to make a dance-floor.

Christos was lounging idly, watching the preparations. At the sound of their voices, he straightened and came towards them, an expression of pleasure on his good-looking face. He spared a word and a smile for Marianthe, but it was obvious his eagerness was all for Chryssanti.

'I was afraid you would not be back in time,' he told her as she greeted him with a greater reserve than she had shown hitherto.

'What's going on?'

'Marcos has invited a band of local musicians on board to play for dancing. They are a very popular group.'

Marianthe was delighted. 'Come on,' she urged Chryssanti. 'Let's go and decide what to wear.'

Chryssanti demurred a little as she followed the other girl. 'I'm not sure I want to dance.'

'Not want to dance?' Marianthe was incredulous. But what Chryssanti really had in mind was Christos's evident enthusiasm. He would be bound to ask her for a dance. She could hardly refuse. But it would only lead to more trouble with Dimitri. She decided to confide in the other girl. After all, Marianthe knew all about the heartache she'd endured four years ago, when she'd fallen in love with Christos, only to discover that he was engaged to be married. And she knew too of the attitude Dimitri had taken at the time.

'I do see your problem,' Marianthe said as they made their way to their cabins. 'But I don't see why you should miss all the fun just because of something that happened years ago. And it *will* be fun if Marcos has organised it. *Are* you still in love with Christos?' she asked with frank curiosity.

'I'm not sure,' Chryssanti confessed. 'There'd never been anyone before I met him. I was crazy about him, and that's a hard thing to forget.'

'Have you fancied anyone since?'

'N-no. Not really.'

'Then it sounds to me as if you *must* still be in love with him. What a pity he's already married,' Marianthe mourned. 'It would have been nice to have you for a sister-in-law. Of course,' she brightened, 'there's always Dimitri.'

'Dimitri?' What had he to do with anything?

'I mean you could marry Dimitri.'

'Huh!' Chryssanti laughed incredulously.

'What's wrong with him? I *like* Dimitri. He has an understanding so many men lack.'

'Understanding? Dimitri? He doesn't understand about me and Christos. And he doesn't believe that, however I feel, I wouldn't come between Christos and Fortula.'

'You don't think Christos is serious, then?'

'Goodness, no. If I thought that...' Chryssanti became pensive for a moment. Then, 'No,' she decided with a sigh, 'he's just flirting. As for Dimitri,' she laughed again a little strainedly, 'I'd really have to be desperate.'

'Evi doesn't think so.'

'Evi?'

'Evi Lemis, his current girlfriend. Well, I suppose you could call her that, though he only sees her when he's on Skiapelos.'

There was no time for Chryssanti to ponder on this piece of information, for they had reached her cabin. Marianthe's was next door.

'Can I come in and see what you're going to wear?' Marianthe asked. 'I know, let's get ready together. Oh, that would be fun. I haven't dressed for a dance with another girl for ages. I'll bring some dresses and *you* can help *me* decide.'

It *was* fun. Neither girl had ever had a sister, and before her marriage, Chryssanti knew, Marianthe's friends would have been carefully monitored. For a while Marianthe forgot her dignity as a married woman, and Chryssanti was able to push her personal problems to the back of her mind.

'*That* one!' Marianthe said positively when Chryssanti displayed the evening wear she had brought with her. 'It's an absolute must for tonight—that glittery gold thread with your fabulous hair.' And, as Chryssanti slipped the dress over her head and smoothed it down around her hips, 'Mmm, sexy. It makes you look a million dollars.'

The dress certainly did cling lovingly to Chryssanti's generous, shapely contours, leaving little to the imagination. Doubtfully, she regarded herself in the mirror, hoping it didn't make her look too 'fast'.

'And I'll wear this one,' Marianthe decided, settling for black and silver. 'We'll make a good foil for each other.'

'There's one thing,' Chryssanti chuckled as they postured before the long mirrors, 'with all those elderly aunts on board, we won't have much competition—except for Lena, of course.'

'You know what we were saying about you marrying Dimitri?' Marianthe said as they left the cabin.

'What *you* were saying, you mean!'

'Yes, well . . . it would please Grandfather Thalassios no end if you married Dimitri. I mean, Thalassios lost his daughter to an Englishman. But he's got his grandson back. And if you married Dimitri you'd be back in the family fold too.'

'When *I* marry,' Chryssanti said with dark certainty, 'it won't be to please Grandfather Thalassios, or anyone else for that matter. When *I* marry, it will be to please myself.'

'Sometimes pleasing yourself can cause unhappiness to others.'

Chryssanti and Marianthe both swung round to find Dimitri behind them. Neither girl had heard his soft footfalls on the carpeted companionway.

Chryssanti was aware that she had flushed scarlet. How much of their exchange had Dimitri overheard?

'You both look very charming. The moon and the sun,' he commented. He had a hand through the crook of each girl's elbow as they emerged on to the pool deck, and Chryssanti felt his grip tighten as Christos came towards them, with eyes only for her.

'You and Marianthe can look after each other, since neither of you has your proper partner aboard,' Dimitri remarked smoothly. With a deft movement he transferred the other girl from his care to Christos, himself retaining a firm hold on Chryssanti as he drew her towards the dance-floor. Without so much as a by your leave, she thought indignantly, as he took her into his arms and into the mêlée of the dance.

Before they had found their stride, another couple jostled them and Chryssanti found herself flung hard up against Dimitri. The unexpected contact with his stunningly masculine body was disconcerting. She tried to pull away, but with ease he maintained their proximity.

'Relax,' he murmured against her temple, an undercurrent of amusement in his deep voice. 'It is only a dance.'

Only a dance? Yes, maybe, but it was difficult to remain that detached about it when his continued closeness was having the strangest effect on her. His chest was hard against her breasts, his stomach taut against hers. And as they moved to the rhythm of the music his muscular thighs brushed hers like an insidious caress.

It must have been that stupid conversation with Marianthe, Chryssanti thought crossly, that was causing these idiotic sensations, making her self-conscious—and too conscious of him. Yes, that was what she was responding to, plus his undoubted masculinity, his virility. Him, as a person, she was still able to detest, she assured herself.

CHAPTER FIVE

EARLY next morning, while the family were still break-fasting on deck, the *Poseidon* neared the cluster of five islands that was Skiapelos. The nearest and largest of the group was that where Thalassios Mavroleon had his villa.

Like any Greek meal, breakfast was a leisurely affair, but Chryssanti, used to different ways, had already finished eating. Excusing herself from the table, she jumped up and went to lean on the rail to watch their approach.

At first everything looked misty and insubstantial, iridescent in the early sunshine, the craggy hills of the islands looking less and less substantial as they climbed into the hazy sky. Trees and rocks on the lower slopes glistened as though embroidered upon gauze.

But the intensity of the sun increased until it was gloriously warm on Chryssanti's bare arms and legs. Apart from formal occasions like last night, she had practically lived in shorts and T-shirt, a rare occurrence at home.

The little harbour-side settlement, which bore the same name as the islands, was a cluster of squat, whitewashed buildings catching the morning light and backed by craggy olive-clad hills. The small houses climbed away from the sea over the mound that was the ancient town.

Aware suddenly of a presence that seemed to lift the tiny fine hairs on her arm, Chryssanti turned to find Dimitri standing beside her, watching her.

'This,' he said softly as he gestured at the view ahead of them, 'is why, most of the time, we Mavroleons choose to return home like this. Helicopters are for speed and efficiency when necessary. But the yacht makes a real homecoming of it, when we see the islands are still waiting for us. And we hate to leave Skiapelos,' he went on, and once again Chryssanti was struck by the poetic turn of his mind. 'The islands refresh us and give us new energy to face the turmoil of mainland life. They invite us back before ever we are out of sight of them. The author Lawrence Durrell called it "Islomania".'

Chryssanti could well understand the Mavroleons' need to recuperate occasionally. Greeks seemed to squeeze more out of a twenty-four-hour day than most people. They arrived at their offices early in the morning and there were many more hours of work after the siesta period. Self-employed professional men, the Mavroleons were often to be found in their offices as late as nine or ten at night.

She had been silent for a long time, deep in thought. Life on these lovely isolated scatterings of islands in the level sea, simple though it might be, could very well be content.

'Do you find our affection for our homeland ridiculous?' Dimitri asked. He sounded as if he might be regretting opening his heart to her so freely.

'Heavens, no,' she hastened to assure him. 'I'm used to it. Uncle Domenicos is just the same. He says that every exiled Greek, no matter how rich his new life has made him, still remains fiercely patriotic. I've listened to Uncle Dom talking for hours, with real tears in his eyes, about Greece and the Greeks.' She shuddered a little. 'He says he hopes to come back to Greece to die.'

The rattle of the *Poseidon*'s anchor chain dispelled morbid thoughts.

'Do we still have to ride up from the harbour on donkeys?' Chryssanti asked Dimitri, remembering the service the proudly independent inhabitants liked to offer their patrons, the wealthy Mavroleons.

'The custom *is* still observed,' he said with a little frown, 'by those who feel able to do so. But if you dislike the idea you can remain aboard until the yacht anchors in the new harbour on the far side of the island.'

'I *don't* dislike the idea,' she said quickly. She didn't want him to think she was belittling the tradition. 'I've always remembered it as being rather fun.'

Christos had made it so, she recalled, by his amusing commentary on the sights they passed along the way. And she had been pleased and flattered by his attention. There would be no ride with Christos today. Dimitri would see to that, as he had seen to it last night that she danced with no one but himself or the occasional elderly uncle. Remembering Christos's lowering looks, she felt uneasy. She knew she was not the only one who had noticed his sullen moodiness and its cause. Once or twice she had thought he was on the point of cutting in, and she had dreaded a scene.

She almost wished she *could* find an opportunity to talk to Christos on his own and tell him firmly that his behaviour was causing comment and that for everyone's sake it must stop.

Half an hour later the launch took the first party ashore, wending its way through the brightly painted fishing caiques that thronged the lagoon-like harbour, glassy still and mirroring the high blue sky. The people of Skiapelos, Dimitri told her—again in spite of the

wealthy Mavroleons' patronage—still earned their living
from the sea.

With Dimitri's hand supportively at her elbow,
Chryssanti crunched her way across the white-pebbled
beach to where a group of donkeys and their attendants
awaited the visitors. Slowly, the donkeys' hoofs ringing
on the cobbles, they made their way uphill, through
narrow streets lined by asymmetrical flat-roofed houses,
interspersed at intervals by tiny blue-domed churches.
Doorways of mahogany or brilliant blue were adorned
with brass hand-shaped knockers, and there were flowers
everywhere, some growing right out of the walls and
rock.

'Oh,' Chryssanti exclaimed, 'it smells just the way I
remember.' She wrinkled her nose appreciatively. 'What
is it? Flowers, cooking, the sea...'

'And dung.' Wryly Dimitri finished the analysis for
her.

She laughed. She was discovering that—whatever else
he lacked—Dimitri had a delightful sense of humour.

Not that he seemed to lack much, she acknowledged
wryly—wealth, position, good looks, a many-faceted
character and, not least, an undoubted charisma that
would devastate any woman whose heart was not already given.

They passed through the hub of the little town, a tiny
square dominated by an enormous and very beautiful
plane tree. Here dark-clothed men sat gossiping com-
fortably to the clack of ancient backgammon pieces and
sipping the thick, sweet Turkish coffee so popular in
Greece. A cat, which surely must also be male, stretched
luxuriously in the hot morning. The womenfolk, mean-
while, sat outside their houses peeling potatoes, rear-
ranged the dust with brooms that could have been

pantomime props or bustled to and fro on countless errands.

'Something else that doesn't change,' Chryssanti commented. 'Male privilege. It's very different in England.'

'You like England?' Dimitri asked.

'I was born there,' she said simply. 'I've lived there all my life. To me it's home, the way Skiapelos is home to you.'

'So you wouldn't consider leaving it permanently? You wouldn't consider marrying a . . . a foreigner?'

She thought she knew what he was hinting at, and she answered sharply, 'I might—if he was the *right* foreigner!'

Beyond the precincts of the little town, their route took them through open countryside. Wild flowers of every colour fought for space against trees and rough grass. Overhead, swallows played endless games of tag in the cloudless blue sky, and the ever present buzzing of cicadas registered their approval of a perfect day.

On the far side of the island the going was less precipitous, and here was Thalassios Mavroleon's white villa overlooking the larger man-made harbour.

'It hasn't changed,' Chryssanti said as memories flooded back of the last time she'd seen the blindingly white buildings, its doors and windows traditionally outlined in blue.

'Some things *are* unchanging,' Dimitri said, 'and it is good that it should be so.' He was looking at her rather oddly, she thought, as he went on, 'But too much clinging to the past can be a mistake.' Again she thought she knew what he was implying, but this time she bit back an angry retort and she was glad the ride was ended.

Inside as well as out, the villa was just as Chryssanti remembered it: wide halls with long windows open to the sun on all sides. On the pristine white walls hung Old Masters, and illumined niches featured sculptured figures. Graceful archways invited the eye through room after perfectly proportioned room.

It was pleasant to find that she had been given the elegant suite of rooms she remembered from her previous visit. Furnished with expensive simplicity, the sitting-room overlooked a shady, vine-covered patio. The bedroom possessed a balcony with a pleasing view of the deep blue water of the harbour. Silver-grey and olive knolls rose from the shore, growing into steeply rising purple hills.

In the en suite bathroom she showered and changed into a full-skirted cream summer dress, exquisitely embroidered around the deep V-neck. Grandfather Thalassios, she recalled, did not approve of women in shorts or trousers, and though she thought him unbearably old-fashioned, as a visitor to his home it was only courtesy to observe his tastes.

Marianthe stuck her head round the door of Chryssanti's bedroom.

'Come on, time to meet the old tyrant!' she said facetiously. In reality, Chryssanti knew, both Marianthe and Lena were fond of the autocratic old man.

As was the Mavroleon custom, the family were gathered in the marble tiled reception hall with its high ceiling and slim Doric columns.

Chryssanti was beginning to think that time stood still in these islands, for Thalassios Mavroleon had not changed either in the past four years. Still as upright, still as handsome with his noble profile, curling white hair and flashing dark eyes, he dominated the assembly, receiving his relations with all the air of royalty greeting his serfs. Dimitri was a lot like him to look at, Chryssanti realised, looking from one to the other, though Dimitri's features were cast in a leaner, more aquiline mould.

As though he felt her eyes upon him, Dimitri came towards her.

'Come and renew your acquaintance with your grandfather,' he invited.

'I planned to,' she told him, and then, a trifle irritably, because he was always hovering at her side, 'and I don't need a bodyguard. I'm not frightened of him.'

Dimitri was thick-skinned too, she seethed, as he ignored her remark and steered her towards Thalassios.

'You remember Chryssanti, *Poppa*? Aunt Irini's daughter?'

'I never forget a member of my family,' Thalassios told him. Flashing dark eyes under shaggy brows regarded Chryssanti. 'You have grown into a beautiful young woman. Is that not so, Dimitri?' And Chryssanti blushed as Dimitri confirmed his grandfather's opinion. But perhaps he wouldn't dare disagree. 'While you are here,' Thalassios went on, 'we must talk about your future.'

'My future is taken care of,' she said hastily.

'By Domenicos Theodopoulos? So I have heard. Nevertheless, we shall talk. But first the christening.' And with a graceful nod of the white head, she found herself dismissed.

'He still likes to rule the roost,' she observed to Dimitri as they moved away.

He smiled. 'Yes, he is still very much the autocrat. The only person who dares to argue with him is his wife.' He nodded towards a tall, graceful but frail-looking woman with iron-grey hair and a gentle face, talking at that moment to Lena.

'His wife? I thought he was a widower?'

'He was married three times. He divorced Tina, his second wife, *your* grandmother and Domenicos Theodopoulos's sister. If you remember, that was the cause of the feud between my grandfather and Domenicos.' And, as Chryssanti nodded, he went on, 'Rallia, *Poppa*'s third wife, had been dead two years last time you came to Skiapelos. And when Thalassios and Domenicos made up their feud, Tina came back and they were remarried. And they are very happy.'

'So she's my *real* grandmother,' Chryssanti stared wistfully at the older woman.

'And she is looking forward to meeting *you*. Needless to say, she adores your brother.'

'Yes, where is Stephen?' Chryssanti looked around the crowded room. 'I thought he'd be here.'

'He has another week at school, on the mainland, before the summer holidays.'

'Well!' Chryssanti exclaimed in exasperation. 'I wish I'd known. I could have gone to see him while I was in Athens.'

Dimitri shrugged.

'If I had known you wished to do so... But I thought, as you had not bothered to visit him in four years...'

'I didn't want to come back to Greece,' she said shortly. 'My memories weren't very happy ones, as you well know.'

'No?' he enquired with mild irony. 'And yet you seem to have clung to those memories, nevertheless. I...'

'I'd like to meet my grandmother,' she interrupted with more haste than politeness. She didn't want to cover *that* ground again. Without waiting for him, she moved

towards Tina Mavroleon. To her surprise, this time he
did not follow her, and it was Lena who performed the
introductions.

It was a very moving encounter for both grandmother
and granddaughter.

'Irini's daughter!' Tina Mavroleon exclaimed softly,
a blue-veined hand on each of Chryssanti's shoulders.
'This is a happy moment for me. I saw a beautiful young
woman talking with Dimitri, but I had no idea. The way
he was looking at you, I thought you were his latest
girlfriend.'

'Heavens, no!' Chryssanti laughed. 'Far from it. I'm
afraid Dimitri disapproves of me. You must have mis-
taken his expression.'

'I want to know all about you,' Tina told her, 'your
life until now and everything you can tell me about Irini.'
She sighed. 'About the lost years.' She slipped a hand
through Chryssanti's arm. 'But we cannot talk here in
this crowd. Walk in the grounds with me, child?'

Chryssanti went willingly. She was not of an un-
sociable disposition, but she did find the Mavroleon
family gatherings somewhat overwhelming. As the new-
comer to their ranks, she had a feeling of being on trial,
the cynosure of all eyes.

'This is one of my favourite places,' Tina told her
granddaughter as they left the villa's more formal gardens
and passed through a small gateway into an untended
area of crooked olives. 'I come here when I want to be
alone and think.'

To suit the older woman's pace they strolled slowly,
arm in arm, between the gnarled trees, while Chryssanti
tried to give her grandmother a summary of the last
twenty-two years.

They both shed tears as Chryssanti spoke of Irini's death.

'That was the thing I found hardest to forgive Thalassios,' Tina confided, 'the way he cut our daughter right out of his life. We had been divorced years before, of course, when Irini was still a child. And I was out of Greece when she ran away with your father. I did not know where she had gone or how to find her. By the time Domenicos discovered her whereabouts, neither my health nor hers permitted travel. We wrote, of course, but after all the years we were like strangers.'

'I don't know how you managed to forgive Grandfather Thalassios anyway,' Chryssanti said. 'The way he divorced you for another woman! Then kept Mum with him. And yet you came back to him.'

'I always loved him,' Tina Mavroleon said simply. 'I found that nothing could change that. You'll under-stand one day, Chryssanti. When you *really* love someone, you can forgive them anything. Remember that, child.' She looked at her watch. 'Goodness, we have been gone almost half an hour.' She wiped her eyes. 'I must get back to the villa.' A shaky little laugh. 'It still feels strange to me to be the hostess there once more.'

'I think I'll stay here for a bit,' Chryssanti said. She still felt very emotional herself. 'I don't think I can face all those people again for a while. You said this was a good place to think, and I feel I've got a lot to think about.'

It was peaceful under the olive trees, a peace con-ducive to thought. She'd spoken the truth when she'd said she had things to think about. Principally it was Christos and his attitude towards her. Frankly, her own reaction confused her. It was flattering, of course, to know that he found her attractive, but there was no pleasure in the flattery, only an uneasy guilt mingled with compassion for his young wife and a feeling of—yes— disappointment in Christos himself. Somehow he was falling short of the heroic qualities with which her memory had imbued him.

As she walked slowly on, dusk shadowed the grove but a full, serene moon sailed overhead. Chryssanti's aimless wandering took her down worn, lichen-encrusted steps into a hollow place of fallen marble stones, the remains perhaps of some old, forgotten temple.

If this were England, she mused, she would have felt nervous, alone in this place of mossy marble and encroaching gnarled fairy-tale trees. But there was no sense of fear. She felt rather that if anything lurked here it was a benign spirit. She sat down on a cluster of exposed roots, leaned back against the tree and listened to the soft rustlings of its moon-silvered leaves.

'So you have found the Garden of the Gods!' Somehow it was no surprise that Dimitri had come in search of her. 'Your grandmother said I should find you here.'

'And I suppose you thought you'd find Christos here, too,' she said bitterly.

'No,' his deep voice told her quietly. 'Christos is talking with our grandfather.'

'Then why follow me?' she demanded. 'Am I not allowed time to myself? I stayed out here because I wanted to be alone, to think.'

'And to grieve?' He had moved closer as she spoke and the moonlight showed him the traces of tears still on her cheeks. 'What cause have you for grief, Chryssanti?' he enquired gently.

'Nothing fresh. It's just that Grandmother and I were talking about my mother. It brought it all back, that

dreadful time when she was dying.' She smiled at him
wanly. 'I'm all right now, but I didn't feel like social-
ising any more tonight.'

'Would *my* society also be unwelcome?'

To her surprise, she found that it wouldn't. Dimitri
might anger her sometimes, but she was never bored in
his company.

'You...you can stay if you want to,' she told him.
And as he lowered his large frame to share her root
complex she said, 'You called this the Garden of the
Gods. Why?'

'It has always been called that, as long as I can remember. Apparently it was here before the villa—the
private temple maybe of some Ancient Greek. It pleases
my grandfather to keep it this way.'

He fell silent then, and Chryssanti couldn't think of
anything to say either.

'Are you...?'

'Did you...?'

They turned towards each other at identical moments,
the movement bringing them into accidental contact.

'S-sorry!' Chryssanti stammered strangely shaken by
the encounter. 'You first.'

But, whatever Dimitri had been about to say, it seemed
he had forgotten it. His eyes searched her face. Was it
the moonlight that gave a strange gleam to their dark
depths? She couldn't imagine what he was thinking, and
for some reason she felt herself colour, yet she couldn't
look away.

'Chryssanti!' He didn't appear to have moved, and
yet suddenly she was in his arms and he was kissing her
with a demanding intensity, his hands holding her close.
For an instant she stiffened but then, as his lips persisted, she felt a contraction, pleasurable but oddly

painful within her. Then she was kissing him back with an eagerness she couldn't hide.

His clasp tightened, constricting her breathing, and as her lips parted in a little gasp for air his tongue invaded their soft, moist warmth, probing delicately, disturbingly.

Sharp, sweet urgency coursed through her, as though some central core of her, untouched and dormant until now, had sprung into ecstatic, quivering life.

'Chryssanti,' he murmured her name against her lips, 'I do not like to think of you grieving alone. I do not like to think of you being unhappy. You were made for joy,' his voice became husky, 'for loving.' He renewed his kisses and his hands began to caress her body, his touch warm through the light material of her dress. Chryssanti was shocked by the force of sensuality surging through her. In the whole of her life she had never known sensations like this. She marvelled that it should be Dimitri of all people who was making her feel this way.

Her body shook in his arms and desperately she clung to him, afraid he would stop, her soft mouth and her body both responding willingly to him. She wanted to be closer to him. She wished he would pull her down on to the dry, sun-bleached grass and press his full length to her.

Fingers trembling, she fumbled two of his shirt buttons undone and slid her hand inside, feeling his chest hair rough and sensuous beneath her palm. At her touch he shuddered suddenly, then went very still. The next moment, to her dismay and astonishment, he had put her away from him.

Again his eyes were intent on her face, as though he would look into the very depths of her soul. Tawny eyes, brown pools in her pale face, met his with an unspoken plea. But it seemed their message was not received. With an impatient sound in his throat he stood up.

'Forgive me. I forgot myself. I think perhaps you did, too? It is time we were getting back. Our absence will have been noticed.'

'Does...does that matter?' she asked tremulously.

'I think so, yes.' He waited for her to stand up, making no attempt to help her. Nor did he touch her as she walked beside him out of the olive grove.

Once or twice she stole a surreptitious glance at his profile, but it told her nothing of his thoughts. Her own were in tumult.

The knowledge that she didn't love Christos any more came with a shock of surprise. Perhaps she never had loved him in the true sense of the word. It had been a youthful idolatry that had encompassed many other things—Greece, the islands, her first awareness of herself as woman rather than child.

But what had brought about this surprising revelation? She hadn't far to look for the answer. Dimitri. She'd only been in his orbit for a few days, but it seemed like years. She had learned so much about him, his interests, his mind, his values. He was a man she could respect, and somewhere along the way she'd realised that Christos couldn't inspire a similar respect.

But surely...she couldn't possibly be in love with Dimitri Mavroleon? You didn't fall out of love with one man and into love with another within the space of days. That was her first thought, quickly superseded by another, the stunning realisation that she *was* in love with him. 'Or at least as near as dammit,' she whispered to herself.

In a dreamlike trance she returned to her suite, wanting to be alone to brood on this unlikely development. But fate had decreed otherwise.

As she entered her suite she was aware almost immediately that someone had been there. A man. There was the aroma of cigar smoke. One of the servants, perhaps, to turn down the bed. But Chryssanti felt sure Thalassios Mavroleon would be displeased to find one of his staff smoking on duty—not that she would report him, of course. But she hoped the bedroom didn't smell of smoke, too. A non-smoker herself, she abhorred the traces it left.

The bedroom door was closed. She was sure she'd left it open. With a sudden feeling of unease she threw it open.

'Christos!' He was sitting on her bed. 'What on earth are you doing in here? Are you mad?'

'Perhaps,' he shrugged. 'It was the only way I could think of to see you without interruption. I *have* to talk to you, Chryssanti.' He stood up and moved towards her.

'Not here.' She didn't particularly want to talk to him. She didn't want to be found in any part of the house with him. But that was preferable to this situation. She must get him out of her suite.

'Yes, here,' he insisted. 'And please do not argue, because I am not leaving until I have said what I came to say.'

Short of making a scene and thus drawing attention to his presence, there was nothing she could do but accede.

'All right. But say what you have to say quickly and then please go.'

She was tense and wary as she faced him, and he stared intently into her face as though choosing what he wanted to say.

'You used not to be so brusque with me,' he said reproachfully. He put his hands on her shoulders. Then, 'Chryssanti, you must know I am in love with you.' It was ironic. If he'd said that four years ago... If he'd said it even four hours ago, it *might* have meant something to her. Now, she realised, it meant nothing, absolutely nothing. And his declaration filled her with alarm.

Gently but firmly she tried to detach his hands, only to meet resistance.

'Don't be silly, Christos,' she told him. 'You can't be in love with me. You've no right to be. You're a married man.'

'Marriage does not necessarily entail love—not in our society. You knew my marriage was an arranged one.'

'You didn't have to go along with it,' she pointed out. 'Marcos didn't, Marianthe and Manoli didn't. At the time you must have been willing.'

'All right.' He shrugged. 'At the time I did not mind much one way or the other. But since Fortula has been pregnant she has been no real wife to me. Nor does she attract me any more. And now you have come back into my life and I know the kind of wife I want, *need*. Chryssanti,' he pulled her closer, 'do you still love me?'

'No, Christos.' She met his eyes squarely, glad that she was able to tell the truth.

'I do not believe you.' He said it savagely.

It didn't occur to her that her unexpected attitude was proving a potent challenge, more so than if she'd regarded him with her former transparent adoration. His normally amiable expression was gone, now his features held bitterness and an intensity of feeling that shocked and frightened her.

'I *know* you feel something for me,' he insisted. 'You made it all too obvious four years ago.'

'That was a long time ago,' she protested. 'I was still only an inexperienced child. It didn't mean anything to you then and it shouldn't now. Please let me go.' But her plea might as well have remained unspoken. His face darkened and his hands gripped tighter.

'You were in love with me. You'd never been in love before and I doubt if you have been since. You are just denying it because of things Dimitri has said to you. You do not have to take any notice of my brother. I will *make* you admit you love me.' With one arm he pulled her hard up against him, his free hand forcing up her chin, his mouth grinding down on to hers. His breath smelt of alcohol and he took no pains to hide his arousal.

Fear gripped Chryssanti. He was strong and they were alone here. The walls of the villa were thick. Even if she'd wanted to draw attention to such a compromising situation, any cries she made for help would be muffled. She must fight her own battle.

But her tightly closed mouth and her resistance cost her dear as she felt his teeth break the skin on her lower lip. With a strength born of anger and disgust, she thrust him away from her. Trembling, she faced him.

'Thank heaven you *were* engaged four years ago,' she spat at him. 'Thank heaven you're married—though I pity your wife. For your information, I *am* over that childish crush—because that's all it was. I know now what love really means.'

'And how do you know that?' he demanded vituperatively. 'That first night in Athens, at my mother's villa, the lovelight was still in your eyes when you looked at me. It was unmistakable. What chance has there been for you to put anyone else in my place? I . . .' His voice trailed away and his eyes hardened. 'So that is it! Dimitri! My own brother has stolen your affections from me.'

'D-don't be ridiculous!' Chryssanti paled. Her feelings for Dimitri were too new, too uncertain, too tender to be bruised by Christos's clumsy anger. No one else knew of them. She had only just discovered them for herself. They might never be requited. But if Christos said something to Dimitri, any chance she had at all would be ruined. 'I . . . I told you . . . I've got a boyfriend back home. I . . . I *was* pleased to see you that night, at Tassia's villa. But that's all it was, pleasure at seeing an old friend— a relation.' She moved towards the door of the suite, held it open. 'Now, please go,' she begged.

For a moment as he strode towards her, she thought he was going without any further protest, but on the threshold he pulled her roughly against him, kissing her with a hard, violent force. She struggled but her efforts only made him tighten his bruising grip. Then, without releasing her, he stared into her face.

'Think about this very carefully, Chryssanti. We Greeks do not like to be rejected.'

As he released her and stepped into the corridor, thankfully she made to close the door, then stopped, leaning on it for support as she stared into the face of Dimitri Mavroleon. His eyes held a chill loathing and she shivered under their icy stare.

'D-Dimitri!' Her voice quivered as beseechingly she said his name.

A multitude of impulses besieged her. She wanted to tell him what had happened. She wanted to cry, wanted *him* to comfort her. But it was useless. Explanations, excuses were no good. And she knew, as he turned on his heel and strode away, that he would never believe her again.

CHAPTER SIX

CHRYSSANTI tossed and turned sleeplessly that night. Normally the bed was the essence of expensive comfort. But Chryssanti felt she might as well have been the heroine of the fairy-tale, *The Princess and the Pea*. No matter how thick and luxurious the mattress, she was aware continually of discomfort.

After four years of comparing every man unfavourably with Christos, it had been disconcerting the way she'd suddenly realised she wasn't in love with him. But now she had leisure to think about it, she knew it had perhaps been inevitable. She had matured. She no longer romanticised as she had when a teenager. But above all, reluctantly, she had to admit that her Greek idol had feet of clay.

So why, with all this new-found wisdom, she mocked herself, was she in danger of falling just as hard for Dimitri? It was a situation surely no more conducive to happiness.

Because Dimitri's manner towards her had mellowed of late, it didn't mean he liked her any better. And now even the foundations of a possible friendship between them had been destroyed. For Dimitri had seen Christos leaving her suite with what must have looked like an intimate and passionate farewell. She couldn't decide which of the brothers she dreaded seeing again most.

It was a sober, still thoughtful Chryssanti who joined the family party next morning—the day of Nikki's christening. And she was grateful that Lena was too preoccupied herself to notice her friend's wan looks.

But Dimitri noticed. Or at least he registered her presence among them before looking away, his classical profile set in cold, immobile lines. Well, if that was the way he wanted to play it . . . Chryssanti's lips could firm in just as taut annoyance. It was an annoyance increased by Christos's manner towards her, which she felt certain was for Dimitri's benefit. Christos was friendly and familiar, just as if she had welcomed his presence in her room last night.

Dimitri did not look her way again. He seemed totally absorbed in his conversation with a small, slim woman with glossy black hair—Evi Lemis, Chryssanti discovered. So that was the type of woman Dimitri preferred. It was a depressing thought.

But, however gloomy Chryssanti might feel, the weather did not match her mood. There had been no fear of its not being a good day for the christening. In Greece it seemed every day was a good day. Hot breezes stirred among the olives on the hillside. The air was spiced with a never-failing delicate fragrance. But in the villa's sheltered grounds, sizzling with cicadas, everything was stilled by the sunlight pouring down on it.

Family and guests gathered at the front door of the villa to receive the priest, Pappas Frangoulis, who was riding with flowing beard and black robes on his donkey. Another smaller donkey followed, bearing an elderly woman almost extinguished by her own black robes.

'Who's she?' Chryssanti whispered to Marianthe.

'The *Pappas'* wife.'

'Wife?'

Irini Forster had purposely kept her children in ignorance of much of their Greek heritage. Thus

Chryssanti had no idea that Greek Orthodox priests were allowed to marry. But as Marianthe explained, she saw that it made sense. Like everyone else on the island, Pappas Frangoulis needed sons to help cultivate his land, or earn a living from the sea.

'Dimitri looks very serious, doesn't he?' Marianthe observed to Chryssanti. 'He'll be thinking about his responsibilities, of course.'

'Responsibilities?' She had believed his grim looks to be connected with herself.

'Mmm. He is to be Nikki's *koumbaros*, godfather. It is an honour, you know. It is not just an empty title. It involves a lot, not just on behalf of the child, but its family too.'

When Lena had asked Chryssanti to be one of Nikki's godparents, she'd been delighted. She'd guessed there would be other sponsors, of course. But that there should be only one other! And that one Dimitri! She and Dimitri, jointly responsible for Nikki's welfare! She felt sure Dimitri would not take his responsibilities lightly. But then, neither would she.

The christening was to take place in the villa's private chapel, which was large and similar in architecture to any of the island's churches, its interior decorated in white and gold.

Behind the wooden *iconostasis* separating the sanctuary from the main body of the church, the apse was pierced by a window through which sunlight illuminated the altar and cast a radiance about the head of the priest, clad now in white. The sun shone too on Marcos and Lena as they stood before the priest with their child.

Nikki was dressed in a white gown and around his neck was a *filakto*, or amulet of blue glass eye beads, for extra protection, Marianthe explained, against the forces of evil. It was a strange combination of the religious and the superstitious.

In a glorious baritone, Pappas Frangoulis chanted the simple but solemn ritual Latin and Greek prayers. Then he called for the godparents to step forward, and Chryssanti saw Dimitri's cold stare as she moved to stand at his side. Nervously, she bit on her full lower lip.

'I presume,' he muttered so only she could hear, 'that you are aware of the duties of a godparent? The *moral* responsibilities?'

'Naturally!' Her tone was as frosty as his as she took his implication.

'One can only hope that, by the time Nikki is old enough to observe, you will be able to set him a better example.'

She bit back an indignant rejoinder as Lena placed Nikki in Dimitri's arms. In turn Dimitri handed the child to the priest, who proceeded to immerse him three times in the holy water, at the same time giving him his name.

Nikki, Lena had explained to Chryssanti, was short for Nicolas, the name of his deceased grandfather.

'The first son is always named for his grandfather. Marcos's father was Nicolas.'

'Then why wasn't Marcos called Thalassios?'

'He was. He prefers to use his second name.'

After his total immersion the baby was dressed in new clothes while family and guests gathered around with traditional wishes of *'Na sas zisi'*—'may the child live for you'.

The christening was followed by the inevitable feasting, under the benevolent eye of the *pappas*. And as long as he remained the celebrations would continue.

As godparents, much attention was centred on Chryssanti and Dimitri, throwing them together in an uneasy partnership. Chryssanti longed to get away from his chilling presence, but it would have been a serious breach of etiquette for her to leave, and her tension grew until she had a nagging headache.

'You look pale, Chryssanti. Are you not well?' It was Christos hovering at her side, despite Dimitri's rigid, disapproving proximity.

'I'm all right,' she said shortly, willing him to go away, but he seemed peculiarly insensitive to her mood.

'Have you thought any more about what I said last night?' he asked in a low, urgent tone.

'No,' she told him, and in a way it was true. Her thoughts had not been on his threat. Instead they had been concerned with Dimitri's opinion of her.

'I meant what I said. I shall not give up.'

'Then you'll be wasting your time!' she snapped. Her headache was becoming unbearable and she spoke more loudly than she'd intended, drawing a sharp, assessing glance from Dimitri. 'Please go away, Christos!' she hissed.

His sensual mouth set stubbornly and she stared at him despairingly, her pain making her feel incapable of dealing with what promised to be an awkward situation. Then Dimitri was at her side, a firm hand at her elbow drawing her away from his brother.

'Pappas Frangoulis is leaving, Chryssanti. We should make our farewells and thank him on the family's behalf.' To her surprise his voice was without censure, quiet and calm and oddly soothing to her jangled nerves. And, although she disliked the idea of spreading more dissension between the brothers, suddenly she knew she could not allow last night's misunderstanding to continue. She lifted her eyes to his classic profile.

'I have to talk to you, Dimitri,' she said urgently.

He inclined his dark head.

'Very well, but later, hmm?'

And with that she had to be content. But the delay did nothing for her state of tension as she rehearsed what she would say to him and wondered whether he would accept her account of Christos's behaviour.

The feast had encroached upon the siesta period, and she decided the best cure for her headache was to take advantage of the remaining time.

She hadn't been able to sleep, but at least the rest had cured her headache she thought an hour later as she left the villa and made her way up the hillside towards the site of the old olive grove. She wanted to get the interview with Dimitri over, but she couldn't hang around all day awaiting his pleasure. She would fill in the time by doing something constructive, and for that purpose she was armed with a sketch block and paintbox.

The area beyond the villa's grounds might be uncultivated, but it was a natural flower-garden. Six-leaved terracotta-coloured poppies grew side by side with the more usual blood-red kind, combining with white, yellow and blue anemones in an effect reminiscent of a Turkish carpet—nature imitating art.

Chryssanti made her way through the olive grove to the 'Garden of the Gods', as Dimitri had called it. By daylight it was possible to imagine how it must have looked in its heyday. The sunken area to which the steps gave access must once have been a lawn. Around it would have been flower-beds and pergolas. And in a shady corner she discovered the remains of some elegant statuary.

She sat down on a lichened block of marble and opened her sketchbook.

An hour later, as she surveyed the finished sketch, she admitted defeat.

'It's not quite right,' she muttered aloud.

'But an excellent attempt, nevertheless.'

Chryssanti started to her feet, the jar of paintwater spilling. Absorbed in her exercise, she had been unaware of anyone's approach. An infinitely disturbing figure against the sunlight, Dimitri made her heart race erratically.

The moment she had been rehearsing was upon her and, conscious of a beating excitement, she averted her gaze, returning it to her painting. She had captured the exact red of the soil—a dusky brick-red—and the anguished twistings of the olive trees were faithfully represented. The Greek goddess on her pedestal looked over the scene with just the right expression of aloofness. But...

'What's wrong with it?' she demanded. She did not expect him to know the answer. Her question was only an attempt to delay the moment of confrontation.

Dimitri moved closer, his shoulder brushing hers. He had an extraordinarily compelling aura. She stole a sideways glance at his chiselled patrician features, and her stomach muscles clenched in a violent spasm.

'As I said, it is an excellent attempt. But I doubt the painter has been born yet who can capture the light of Greece in the way Van Gogh rendered the light of Provence.'

It was amazing how often he was right. The liquid clarity of the light gave no half-tones, making atmosphere, depth and perspective hard to reproduce.

'Perhaps when I translate it into oils?' she said doubtfully.

'Perhaps.' With a wave of his hand he dismissed the matter of the painting. 'But we have other things to discuss.' He gestured to her to reseat herself, then lowered himself to the ground, stretched out at her feet, his dark head so close to her knee that, had she wanted to, she could have reached out and touched the thick springy waves of hair.

As though afraid she might succumb to the impulse, nervously she clasped her hands in her lap. She must be insane to feel this intensity of emotion about a man who couldn't make up his mind whether to be a friend or an enemy.

'You said you wanted to talk to me,' he reminded her.

'Yes. But ... but I don't know where to begin.'

Dimitri had no such doubts. He went straight to the heart of things.

'Suppose you begin with Christos's visit to your room last night?'

'I know how it must have looked,' she said desperately, 'but please believe me, Dimitri, I didn't invite him there. I didn't *want* him there. And I certainly didn't want him to kiss me like that.' She waited in anguished silence for his reaction, and when none was forthcoming, 'Dimitri?'

'Strangely enough, I *do* believe you.' There was an odd note in his voice, and his gaze was intent on the activity of his fingers as they plucked at the sun-dried grass.

'Oh, thank goodness!' The intensity of her relief astonished her. 'I ...'

'Perhaps I am a fool to do so. Perhaps it is just that I *want* to believe you, but ...' He pivoted on his elbow and looked up into her face just as she leaned forward, anxious to convince him of her sincerity.

'Dimitri, I...'

As dark eyes locked with tawny ones, he stretched out his free hand and caught hold of hers, drawing her down beside him. At his proximity she was shocked by the force of the sensuality that surged through her. It was beyond all her experience.

'I *want* to believe you, Chryssanti,' he reiterated, his tone urgent. 'You do not know how much.'

'Why?' she dared to ask. It was only a breath of sound. 'Why is it so important to you? Is it... is it because of Fortula? Because I...'

'No! It is because of *you*, Chryssanti.' The deepened cadences of his tone kept her eyes riveted on his. 'I am sorry,' he went on, 'that things have worked out so unsatisfactorily for you. I know only too well how painful it can be to love with no hope of happiness.'

A sudden stab of pain distracted Chryssanti from the fact that Dimitri thought she was still in love with Christos.

'Evi?' she asked.

He looked at her blankly.

'Evi Lemis. Marianthe said...' His laughter, albeit wry mirth, interrupted her speculations.

'No. Evi is good company but she means nothing more to me and she knows it. She asks for nothing more.'

'Then I suppose you mean your fiancée? I believe she died. I'm sorry.'

'That was many years ago. Before I first met you.' He sounded impatient. Then, 'Chryssanti, I came to find you to tell you that Christos has been recalled to Athens.' He watched her face closely. 'Fortula has been taken seriously ill. At the very least she may lose the baby— at the worst her own life.' And, as Chryssanti's eyes grew large with dismay, he went on harshly, 'So you see, Christos may yet be free to marry again—to marry *you*.'

'What a perfectly horrible thing to say!' Chryssanti jumped to her feet. Her eyes blazed and her lips trembled. Dimitri rose, too. His lips were drawn into bloodless lines as she went on, 'Is that what you think I'd want? Well, I'm glad to know just where I stand with *you*—just what you really think of me.' As he moved towards her, his hands spread in a would-be-placating gesture, she struck out at him.

He captured her flailing fists and held them against his chest. His face was inches from hers as she glared up at him, all other emotions forgotten in her fury.

'I hate you!' she whispered. 'I hate you!' But it was a dangerous hatred, too akin to love.

'*Theos mou!* Do you think I *want* to believe you are waiting to step into another woman's shoes?'

'Then *don't* believe it,' she told him vehemently, struggling to free herself. 'And don't you ever accuse me of anything so...so...' Words failed her. 'I wouldn't wish harm to a single hair of Fortula's head. To wish anyone's life away would be wicked...wicked!' As her voice broke on a sob, Dimitri gathered her into his arms and to her own astonishment she did not resist him.

'She may not die,' he said soberly, and his words scarcely registered against the impact of the man himself. A strange restlessness stirred inside her. But he was still speaking. 'Let us hope and pray she does not die. Chryssanti...' he hesitated, 'I think this shock may bring Christos to his senses. Deep down I believe he *does* love Fortula. I only hope he has not realised it too late.' When Chryssanti made no reply, he continued, 'I know it is easy to say this and much harder to perform. But could you not *try* to put Christos out of your mind now? Out of your heart?'

She could feel an odd tension in his body and she raised her head to look at him. The bone structure of his face was so beautiful, she thought bemusedly. She felt a longing to trace its lineaments with her fingers.

'But I don't . . .'

'Oh, I believe you when you say you did not mean to encourage him. Your anger with his persistence today was so obviously genuine.' But his dark, handsome face was still troubled. 'But, loving him as you do, the temptation must be very great. You are only human, and you must be very unhappy. Perhaps it would be better—for everyone concerned—if you cut short your visit.'

'No!' The explosive negative brought him up short. 'No, Dimitri,' she said more quietly. 'I'm *not* unhappy—at least, not about Christos. And I'm not in love with him. Oh, I thought I was once,' she went on hurriedly as he seemed about to interrupt, 'but I've outgrown that childish infatuation, I promise you.'

Dimitri's face was undergoing the strangest transformation, from concern to relief, from relief to a sudden new doubt.

'Then you have made up your mind—about the boyfriend at home? What was his name? Terence? You will marry *him*?'

'I haven't made up my mind about anything,' Chryssanti told him. How *could* she make up her mind about the future when one option at least was still unclear to her? 'I've only just finished my studies. I have my career to consider. I'm not in any hurry to marry *anyone*.' But as she said it she knew it was not strictly true.

She was still clasped in Dimitri's arms and now, gently, she freed herself, though she was disappointed to meet no resistance, and just as disappointed that he seemed to accept her statement. He even seemed interested.

'You want a career? As what?'

'Something to do with art. Preferably with an art publisher,' she told him, as previously she'd told Lena.

'And does this have to be in England?'

'I suppose not. But it would certainly be easier. I don't speak any foreign languages.'

'English is a universal language,' he said thoughtfully. 'Suppose I were to use my influence to get you a position with a firm of publishers in Athens—would you consider it?'

Chryssanti was gripped by a sudden elation. She knew that she didn't really want to go back to England. Because if she did she was unlikely to see Dimitri again, except perhaps at family reunions. And that wouldn't be enough. Not nearly enough.

'Of course I'd consider it,' she told him. Then, with fluttering pulses, 'But why should you take all that trouble on my behalf?'

'I would like you to stay in Greece, Chryssanti.' There was something in the way he said it which made it impossible for her to avoid his eyes.

'Oh!' It came out as a croak. She longed to ask why again, but dared not. 'I ... I'd like to stay,' she added after a long silence in which it seemed he did not intend to say any more.

He gave a nod of satisfaction.

'That is settled, then. When we return to Athens I will make enquiries.' He looked down at her forgotten sketching materials. 'Have you finished painting for today?' And, as she nodded, he bent and picked up the sketchbook and paints, extending his other hand to her.

It seemed natural and right to put her hand into his and walk with him through the garden. But their intertwined fingers, the occasional pressure of his that seemed to convey a certain intimacy, was disturbing too, suspending her breath.

'My grandparents won't be very happy about it,' she said a little unevenly. 'They feel they've already lost one grandchild to Greece.'

'The world is very small,' he observed. 'You will be able to visit them often. Besides, you may not wish to stay in Greece forever. You may wish to move on.'

'Yes.' He sounded so confident of it that her heart sank, depression swamping her again. Perhaps he was just being polite when he'd said he would like her to stay. After all, his offer of help with her career was no more than any relation would do one for another.

As they left the grove of twisted olives, they met Lena and Marcos coming in the other direction, strolling slowly, their arms wound around each other. They looked blissfully happy, and Chryssanti was aware of an aching sensation around her heart. It must be wonderful to love someone and be as sure of their love as of your own.

'How do you like the Garden of the Gods, Chrys?' Lena asked. 'It's one of our favourite places, isn't it, Marcos?' As the couple's eyes met they were full of amused and affectionate recollection. Chryssanti could well imagine what might have happened between these two in that enchanted place. And she found herself wishing with all her heart that *Dimitri* had made love to *her* there.

What would he be like as a lover? As he talked to Marcos she had opportunity to observe him, to imagine that lean, muscular body pressed to hers in urgency, in dominance, his mouth taking hers in hungry, demanding impatience. The imagery was so vivid that she shuddered violently.

'Surely you are not cold, Chryssanti?' Dimitri placed an arm about her shoulders and looked enquiringly into her face.

'No.' She forced a smile. 'Just someone walking over my grave.'

Lena was looking at her assessingly.

'I don't believe you heard a word Marcos said,' she accused.

Blushing, Chryssanti admitted it.

'You were *miles* away,' Lena continued wonderingly. 'And you had such an odd expression on your face. I can't imagine what you were thinking.' Curiously, 'Did Dimitri tell you about Christos? About Fortula being ill?'

'Oh, yes. And I do hope everything will turn out all right. But I wasn't thinking about that,' she hastened to add. She sought to change the subject. 'I'm sorry I wasn't listening. What *was* Marcos saying?'

'That we are going across to our own island tomorrow. You remember I told you we are building our own summer retreat there? We wondered if you would like to come with us?'

'Oh!' Chryssanti said doubtfully. Right now she didn't want to be away from Skiapelos, or, more accurately, from Dimitri. 'Wouldn't you rather be alone?'

'Dimitri is invited, too,' Lena said, a strange emphasis in her voice that was totally lost upon Chryssanti as she pondered how she could accept now without seeming too eager and giving cause for speculation.

Dimitri eased the way for her.

'I should be glad of your presence, Chryssanti, if you will take pity on me. I like going to the island. But when these two lovebirds get away from their responsibilities they are tedious company. They only have eyes for each other. So, will you come?'

Agreement reached, the two couples went their separate ways, Marcos and Lena into the grove, Dimitri and Chryssanti towards the villa.

'I can guarantee that you will enjoy yourself,' Dimitri assured her. His arm was still around her shoulders. 'In fact, I will make it my business to see that you do.'

They were just within sight of the villa when he stopped in his tracks and turned her towards him so that he could look into her eyes. His own were soft, so warm and gentle it took her breath away. 'I feel I have a lot to make up to you, Chryssanti. I have not always been kind to you. Earlier you told me you hated me. It is no more than I deserve if you do.'

He was holding her so lightly that she could have freed herself, but she didn't.

'I don't hate you,' she said huskily. And yet once upon a time she had. How long ago that seemed, another lifetime, another person. Some deep, secret part of her had been changed. She would never be the same again.

'No, thank goodness. I believe you do not.' His grave tone lightened suddenly. 'Let us look on tomorrow as a new beginning, Chryssanti. From now on, let us try to get to know each other as friends rather than enemies?'

As she stared into his dark eyes, trying to read their unfathomable message, it seemed to Chryssanti that the very air around them pulsated with sexual excitement. There was a gnawing ache in the pit of her stomach and she was dizzy with desire for him, so that she had almost forgotten his initial question when he asked, 'Do you agree?'

Speechlessly she nodded, still drowning in his gaze. For a moment he retained his hold on her. Then gently he turned her from him, urging her towards the villa once more, his arm dropping from her shoulders as they walked on. For her that moment of separation was like the sudden end of a beautiful piece of music, broken off for no reason, the end of something hardly begun.

CHAPTER SEVEN

'YOU and Dimitri seem to be getting on much better,' Lena observed next day as she and Chryssanti waited by one of the villa's limousines for the two men to join them.

'Yes,' Chryssanti said slowly. There was still an element of doubt in her mind. 'I think I've finally managed to convince him I don't want to break up Christos's marriage.'

'I should think so!' Lena exclaimed indignantly. 'It would have saved a lot of trouble if he'd asked *me*. I could have told him you weren't like that.' She looked shrewdly at her friend. 'I believe you're over Christos, aren't you?' Chryssanti nodded. 'I thought so. Once or twice I've sensed—or perhaps it was wishful thinking—that Dimitri was interested in you himself?' And, as Chryssanti did not volunteer any remark, 'Anyway, during these next few days I hope you'll have a lot of time to yourselves and then,' she shrugged, 'who knows?'

Chryssanti knew her face was flushed, and she changed the subject rather hurriedly. 'Don't you mind leaving little Nikki behind?'

'In one way I do,' Lena confessed. 'I'm besotted with him, as you've probably noticed. But I vowed I wouldn't become so maternal that Marcos would suffer. I may sound an unnatural mother, but my husband will always come first with me. And I know Nikki's in good hands with his nurse. Oh, good, here come the men. Aren't we lucky, Chrys, to have such handsome escorts?'

It was obvious that Lena's remark was made for Marcos's benefit. But that meant Dimitri heard it too, and his dark eyes sought Chryssanti's as though he was waiting for her reply. If he had meant less to her she could have replied coquettishly. But the very fact of his masculine appeal to her senses rendered her uncharacteristically tongue-tied and her gaze fell before his. But she did not need to look at him to be aware of his erect, confident carriage, the way his short-sleeved shirt revealed bronzed, muscular arms, while brief shorts did the same for his long, strong legs.

The limousine took them and their luggage down to the harbour. But instead of going out to the yacht as Chryssanti had expected, the men led the way towards a small fishing *caique*.

'Sometimes Marcos likes to live the simple life,' Lena told her when she expressed astonishment. 'It might surprise you to know how rarely rich people can be alone, away from a crowd of servants and employees, business connections.'

'Does it bother you?' Chryssanti asked curiously. Though she did not dwell on the subject, she had wondered from time to time what it would be like to have to adjust to the wealthy life-style that would inevitably be hers some day, when Domenicos Theodopoulos died.

'Sometimes,' Lena confessed. 'But I wouldn't change places with anyone. Not because of the money, but because Marcos is the most wonderful man in the world. I do hope you'll feel that way about someone again some day.'

For a moment Chryssanti was tempted to please her friend by confessing that she already did. But it was still too fragile a feeling. And despite her new rapport with Dimitri it might come to nothing.

Slowly the broad-bottomed craft made its way over the flax-blue sea, towards the little group of four satellite islands which, with the main island, made up the group known as Skiapelos.

'Do the other islands have names?' Chryssanti asked Lena as the *caique* touched the edge of the white sandy beach.

'Only ours.' Lena had been married four years, but she could still blush charmingly. 'Marcos insisted on naming it for me—Helenos.'

It looked a wild little rock, with its sloping beach and broom-covered hillocks. Marcos helped Lena to step ashore. But Dimitri, in a sudden apparent exuberance of spirits, swept Chryssanti right off her feet and carried her several yards up the beach. He set her down, looking quizzically into her flushed and laughing face. His breathing, only a little more rapid than usual, fanned her cheek.

'Our new beginning, Chryssanti?' he asked with a quizzical lift of dark brows. 'Laughter, not tears? Friends, not enemies?'

Tinglingly aware of him and of the incredible, effortless sensuality he exuded, she nodded wordlessly and he let her slide to her feet, taking her hand in his instead.

A short climb took them to the highest point of the island, the plateau where Marcos had chosen to erect his house.

'I thought it was still being built,' Chryssanti said as Marcos and Lena came abreast of them. 'But it looks finished to me.'

'It is habitable,' Marcos told her. 'But there are one or two refinements I wish to add.'

'Nothing but the best for Marcos!' Dimitri teased him.

'Nothing but the best for *my wife*,' Marcos corrected, making Lena blush again.

Marcos and Lena's summer retreat was a pocket villa, a plaything built by a wealthy man for his wife to keep house. Here, without servants to intrude on their intimate moments, they could capture the illusion of self-sufficiency. Here Lena could cook and clean while Marcos tended the rocky garden and carried out the embellishments his heart was set on.

A swift guided tour revealed living-room, master bedroom and two guest-rooms set about a central *atrium*, while an adjacent wing contained a small but efficiently equipped kitchen. Lena immediately set about preparing a simple but appetising lunch.

They ate outside. The terrace, surprisingly, commanded an inland view of the island, a steep gnarled knob of a place. But, though the barren hillside was almost completely without vegetation, exquisite wild flowers bloomed everywhere, rooted in the crannies of the rocks.

'We thought it would make a change,' Lena explained. 'In Greece, one is never far from water.'

'I don't think I'd ever tire of looking at the sea,' Chryssanti said wistfully. 'Back home, going to the seaside involves quite a journey.'

'Do you *have* to go home, Chrys?' Lena asked. 'We visit my parents, of course, but I don't think I could bear to go back permanently to that cold, damp climate.'

'I too am trying to persuade her to stay,' Dimitri put in before Chryssanti had decided what answer to make. Briefly he related their conversation about the publishing house in Athens.

'Though I find it strange,' he went on, 'that she should wish for a career. She is half-Greek, after all, and most

Greek women prefer the role of wife. You are not Greek, Lena, but it is so with you, too?'

'Oh, yes!' Lena said softly with a melting look at her husband. 'But then, I met the right man.'

Again Chryssanti was aware of Dimitri's gaze resting on her averted profile. She wished she had the courage to meet his eyes boldly, but since yesterday she felt paralysingly shy in his presence.

'And now you have given Marcos a son, you feel you are truly fulfilled?' Dimitri questioned Lena further.

'Not as fulfilled as she will be,' Marcos growled playfully, 'when she has given me two or three more.' And Chryssanti felt envy mingle with embarrassment at the intimacy of the conversation.

As they lingered over their lunch, the day grew steadily warmer, the sun now at its zenith. Marcos gave an exaggerated yawn.

'Siesta time,' he announced, apparently to all in general, but his dark, expressive eyes slanted sideways towards his wife, and yet again Chryssanti saw the lovely, aware colour stain her friend's cheeks. 'Will you two take the siesta?' Marcos asked his guests.

Dimitri looked at Chryssanti.

'What is it to be?' he asked her. 'Siesta? Or would you like to see the rest of the island? Have a swim, perhaps?'

Chryssanti knew she felt far too restless for sleep. She was tremulously anticipating being alone with Dimitri. She was eager to experience the new relationship he had proposed, to know what form he intended it to take. But she was nervous too, fearful of disappointment.

It was strange. If she hadn't come back to Greece she would have gone on in a kind of quiet melancholy, be-

lieving it was Christos she loved. Whereas now there was
the fresh, torturing uncertainty of loving Dimitri.

'I'd enjoy a swim,' she told him. 'That is, unless *you'd*
rather go to bed?'

A stifled chuckle from Marcos made her realise the
interpretation that could be put on her words. On the
defensive immediately, her tawny eyes dared Dimitri to
make something of it.

His face was preternaturally grave as he rose from the
table.

'*Kala!* Good! A swim it is. I will meet you here in ten
minutes. I suggest you wear slacks and stout shoes and
carry your bathing things. The going will be a little rough
until we reach the beach.'

'There...there isn't any—er—wildlife, is there?'
Chryssanti asked as they left the villa. Lena and Marcos
had already disappeared when, clad in serviceable jeans,
a skimpy T-shirt and the stout shoes he'd called for, she
rejoined Dimitri on he terrace.

He grinned. 'The most ferocious thing you are likely
to encounter is the mosquito.'

'No...no snakes or creepy-crawlies?'

'Not on Helenos,' he said reassuringly. 'The occasional scorpion, perhaps. But, as they keep to small dark
places, we are unlikely to disturb one. And anyway, their
sting is not fatal.'

Rough but manageable paths led over the hillside in
several inviting directions. They moved slowly, in single
file sometimes, and sometimes side by side. Occasionally Chryssanti felt Dimitri's bare arm brush her
own, and the contact brought with it the usual awareness
that was half dread, half wanting.

'I like this island. It is very different here,' Dimitri
said, 'even from Skiapelos, do you not think so?'

She could only agree. On mainland Greece, even on Skiapelos itself, life had a quick rhythm, born of the Greeks' virile nature and energetic curiosity. But no one else lived on this golden brown, stern, craggy island.

'Here one may be alone with the gods and with nature,' Dimitri went on. 'There is time to consider the important things of life.'

'What do *you* consider important?' she asked him curiously. 'I would have thought business came first with all the Mavroleons.'

'Not so,' he contradicted. 'True, we work hard so that we and our families, our dependents, may live. But it is always good to get back to our roots, to the simplicity of our island home. Here there is time to think about the gentler side of life: poetry and literature, nature and . . . love.'

Love. What did *he* mean by love? Chryssanti's heart pounded wildly in her breast at the intimate trend *her* thoughts had immediately taken. She waited for him to enlarge on his theme, but he did not do so. Disappointment mingled with a sensation that was almost relief as they walked on. How inconsistent her feelings for Dimitri were making her—at one moment longing for some sign that perhaps *he* was in love with *her*—the next wondering if she could cope with such a declaration. She loved him, yet somehow she was in awe of him, too.

On the far side of the hill they paused at a deep natural spring to refresh themselves, and Chryssanti tried in vain to capture enough water to quench her thirst.

'Here, let me,' Dimitri said. He cupped large hands which held the water more efficiently than her own and offered them to her mouth. The water, she found, tasted quite unlike water anywhere else, having an invigorating freshness uniquely its own. Or was it the vessel from which she received it?

As she held his hands steady in order to drink the cool liquid, she was vibrantly aware of his closeness. There was an intimacy in the gesture he was performing for her. This was another item to add to her rich store of experience of this man. The coolness of the water, the warmth of Dimitri's hands, the vibrant masculinity of him—all were encapsulated with other sensory perceptions. The heat of the sun, the burnt-sugar smell of wild thyme and a hundred other vegetable scents peculiar to such untamed parts of Greece.

As they moved on again, below them Chryssanti saw a tiny bay, a perfect crescent of sandy beach, almost white against the water, blues ranging from pale turquoise to fountain pen ink. Lazy wavelets lapped gently on the shining newly washed shore.

Suddenly she couldn't wait to be in the sea's silky embrace. She ran down the last slope of the hill, then paused to look about her. A frown creased the perfection of her brow.

'There's nowhere to change!'

'But there is no one here to see you,' Dimitri pointed out. Except for Dimitri himself, she thought wryly. 'And I promise *I* will not look,' he added as though he'd read her thoughts. Ostentatiously he turned his back.

Facing away from him, she scrambled out of her clothes and into the scanty white bikini which was the only swimwear she'd brought to the island. Nervously she peeped over her shoulder to make sure he was keeping his promise, then had to stifle a gasp.

His back still towards her, Dimitri was completely naked. A whirling eddy of feelings was let loose inside her as she let her eyes travel from the broad shoulders downwards. The hard lines of his body narrowed to a trim waistline, sensuous hips and strong legs. He was a truly magnificent mass of bone and muscle, the olive of his skin deepened by the sun, except for the lighter area of flesh on his well-shaped buttocks.

As, totally mesmerised, she watched him, he stepped into a pair of brief black trunks then turned towards her, catching her startled arrested gaze upon him. Although she was discovered, she still could not look away. The sunlight made his bronzed skin gleam, his black hair had the sheen of polished jet.

'Do you like what you see?' he asked teasingly, but she was incapable of replying.

Slowly he moved towards her, his eyes making his own sexual appraisal of her tall, slender figure.

'You do not play fair, Chryssanti!' There was laughter in his voice now, and a glint in his eye that she mistrusted.

'I—I didn't mean...I didn't realise...I thought you...' She'd expected him to have his trunks on under his clothes.

'I've often wondered how *you* would look undressed,' he went on throatily.

'You—you've seen me like this before. And a bikini isn't undressed,' she said. But it might as well have been, the way his dark eyes were devouring her.

'Maybe, but it wouldn't take much to...'

'No, Dimitri, no!' She thrust out her hands in a gesture of rejection, but he continued to advance. She wasn't sure what his intentions were and she didn't wait to find out. Cravenly she turned and fled, over the soft, sugary sand and into the safer embrace of the sea, hearing the soft, threatening pad of his footsteps behind her as she ran.

She plunged into the sea and began a fast overarm crawl. When, finally, tired and breathless, she could swim no further, she surfaced and looked nervously behind her. She was well aware that, with those long limbs and powerful muscles, Dimitri could easily have kept pace with her. It was a shock and, yes, a cause of chagrin, to see his dark sleek head bobbing lazily not far from the point where she had taken to the water. He'd made no attempt to follow her.

With a distinct sense of anticlimax she swam slowly back towards him.

'Do you feel better for that?' he drawled. His sensuous lips were curved in knowing amusement. 'What were you afraid of, Chryssanti, I wonder?'

'I wasn't afraid of anything,' she lied. 'I just felt like working off some surplus energy.'

'You had some surplus energy?' he asked in mock surprise. 'After that long walk? In this heat?' He sounded disbelieving, as well he might.

Trying to walk nonchalantly past him through the shallows towards the beach, Chryssanti staggered a little. Her legs felt decidedly shaky. Not just the weakness they'd begun to feel recently in his company, though that was there too, but also the weakness of extreme fatigue. She *had* overdone it in her wild race through the water.

Dimitri put out a hand to steady her, but he took no further advantage of the situation.

'Wrap your towel around you and we'll find somewhere cool for you to sit and rest, out of the sun.'

'Somewhere cool? Is that possible?'

Apparently it was. Still holding her elbow, his touch far too impersonal for her liking, Dimitri steered her towards the cliff-face where a cleft in the rock, not easily visible to the casual eye, led into a cave. It was the first of a series leading one into another, he told her.

'We used to play here as children. They are quite spectacular, but we will not venture in too far today.'

Daylight penetrated the cave from a chink in the roof, and Dimitri made her sit down on a projecting rock while he pointed out a most unexpected sight.

'Stalactites and stalagmites!' Chryssanti exclaimed. 'How beautiful!'

'Yes,' he agreed, but when she looked at him his eyes were on her rapt face and she gave a convulsive swallow, a fact his keen gaze did not miss.

'You said you were not afraid, Chryssanti. But I believe you *are* afraid—and of me. Why?' He gave her no chance to reply, but went on, 'I am not my brother. And whatever the temptation, I assure you my behaviour is far more circumspect.'

Right now it wasn't circumspection she wanted of him. Despite his protests, he *had* kissed her once or twice. Surely he wouldn't have done that unless she held some attraction for him, however slight. And he *had* mentioned temptation. Was he tempted by her? A wild idea was born in her head, born of a consuming need to know.

'I'm not afraid of you. And you haven't always been so circumspect,' she reminded him throatily. 'What about that night in the Garden of the Gods?'

He inclined his head in acknowledgement of her words.

'True. But as I told you then, I forgot myself and so, I think, did you. I kissed you because you were unhappy. But for a moment you were imagining I was another man. Was that not so?'

'No...' she began.

'Oh, you have since told me you are no longer in love with Christos. But I think it is a recent realisation. That night in the garden I think you still imagined yourself in love with him, and when *I* kissed you, you allowed yourself to believe that I . . .'

'No!' she said again. With great daring, she held his gaze. 'I knew exactly who I was kissing.'

'I see.' She thought his voice sounded a little uneven. 'You seemed to be enjoying the experience?'

'Yes.'

'So I thought . . .'

'I wasn't pretending you were Christos,' she insisted.

'Nor thinking about anyone else?'

'No.'

There was silence for a moment, then he bent towards her, put his hands under her armpits and raised her to her feet.

'I wonder what you would be thinking of, Chryssanti, if I were to kiss you now?'

She dared not tell him.

Continuing to support her with one hand, with the other he raised the still damp red-gold hair from her neck, his hand moving on her nape in a sensuous massage as he bent and put his warm lips to her throat.

She shuddered convulsively and grasped at his shoulders for support as she felt the old insidious weakness assail her knees once more.

As he felt her involuntary reaction, his arms closed about her and he pulled her hard against his chest.

'What exactly do you want of *me*, Chryssanti?' he asked in a low voice.

Against the pounding of his heart her voice was almost lost. 'Don't you know?'

'No,' his voice was harsh. 'You'll have to tell me.'

'I . . . I want you to kiss me . . . properly this time. Not just because you are angry with me. Not because I'm unhappy—and only if you *want* to.'

'Oh, I want to, all right.' She felt a little tremor run through his hard body, then his mouth was claiming hers, her head forced back by the power of his kiss. At the pressure of his thighs against hers, the feel of his hands pressing into her back, a coil of helpless awareness tightened inside her. Her senses were tormented by the masculine odours of his sea-slicked, sun-warmed flesh.

She plunged her hands into the thick, virile hair at the nape of his neck, then ran her hands in quick, restless caresses from his nape to his shoulders, down the long line of his back. As his kiss intensified, she pressed against him. She needed to be as close to him as was humanly possible. Her body arched, she clung to him, shivering convulsively.

And soon kisses were not enough for either of them. His hips moved against her, making her aware of his need, and his hands began to stroke her body, lingering exploringly on her swollen, hardened breasts, the slight curve of her stomach between her hips. At his touch, faint moans of pleasure escaped her and she felt his own desire rising against her.

'Dimitri!' she said pleadingly. She wasn't sure what she was begging for, whether she wanted him to appease the violent need that racked her, or whether she wanted him to exert the control she was fast losing.

Whichever way it was, the sound of her voice seemed to recall him to his senses. He wrenched himself free of her arms and stood a little distance from her.

'*Theos mou*, Chryssanti!' He stared down into her bemused, glazed eyes. 'This must stop. Do you know what you are doing to me? Do you know what you are asking

for? We should not have started this, not here, not now.
I am only human. Come!' He started towards the mouth
of the cave, a jerk of his head indicating that she should
follow him.

Slowly, she did so.

'Do you wish to swim any more?' His voice was harsh
and not quite steady.

Dully she shook her head. She couldn't understand
what had gone wrong. Dimitri had been enjoying kissing
her. She knew that, just as she knew how much he had
been aroused. Now he seemed angry and she didn't know
why.

The way back over the hillside seemed much longer
than it had done coming, probably because of the silence
that lay between them like a barrier. Chryssanti felt a
misery that was too deep for tears. She had forsaken her
natural pride in asking Dimitri to kiss her. She had risked
everything on one throw of the dice, and it seemed she
had lost.

They were within sight of the villa when it happened.

A pace or two behind Dimitri's long stride, lost in
unhappy reflection, head down Chryssanti trudged on,
which was how she saw the sinister shape as it scuttled
into her path and across her foot. Chryssanti was no
coward, but she had a phobia about any kind of 'creepy-
crawlie'—her blanket term for anything that slid or
scuttled. Her stifled scream made Dimitri swing round,
cannoning into her as involuntarily she increased her
pace.

'What the...?'

'A—a scorpion. It ran across my foot. You said we
wouldn't see any.'

His hands on her upper arms steadied her as she
clutched at his shirt.

'It didn't sting you?' he demanded sharply.

'No. But it was horrible—horrible. Such an ugly thing.' Her voice, already unsteady, broke completely. The shock of the incident, trivial though it might seem to him, shattered the numb misery with which she'd received his apparent rejection of her, and she burst into tears.

'Chryssanti!' As he pulled her against his chest, her name was a groan on his lips. 'Stop it. I thought tears were forbidden here, and you know I cannot bear you to weep. You are not hurt. What have you to weep for?'

What indeed? It *was* ridiculous. Just because Dimitri had demonstrated very clearly that he wasn't in love with her. After her experience with Christos, she ought to have known better. And this too would pass, she tried to tell herself.

Shakily she tried to pull free.

'I'm sorry. I'm all right now. I expect it was just the shock. And I'm tired. Perhaps I've had a bit too much sun today.' She knew she was making too many excuses by the way he looked at her. And this was confirmed by his next words.

'There is more to those tears than that. But come.' He put an arm around her waist and swung her into his strong arms. 'I will carry you the rest of the way.'

Chryssanti closed her eyes so that she could not see the angle of his jaw, the way his dark hair curled over his shirt collar. But, though she might be able to quell one sense, she was not so successful with the others. His body was warm and muskily masculine to her nostrils, his breath fanned her face and she could hear the pounding of his heart beneath the thin material of his shirt. Every moment was one of sensual torment.

Lena and Marcos were taking a post-siesta stroll in their garden as Dimitri reached the plateau carrying his burden.

'Goodness!' Lena exclaimed as she rushed towards them. 'What is it, Chrys? Have you had a fall? Are you hurt?'

'No,' Chryssanti said, low-voiced, as Dimitri set her on her feet. 'I'm all right, Lena, honestly. Please don't fuss.' She felt that if anyone gave her sympathy she would burst into tears again. She turned away, intending to make for the villa and the privacy of her room. But Dimitri's voice halted her.

'We will talk about this again later, Chryssanti—when you are rested and in a more rational frame of mind.'

'Th-there's nothing to talk about.' She turned to Lena. 'A scorpion ran over my foot, that's all.' And stiffly to Dimitri, 'I'm sorry I was so silly.'

By dinnertime that evening, Chryssanti had regained her sense of proportion. It had been unrealistic of her to expect a declaration of love from *Dimitri*, of all people. For heaven's sake, she told herself, it was only days since he had been her sworn enemy, dedicated, as he saw it, to saving Christos's marriage.

The fact that Dimitri had kissed her, however much he had been aroused, meant nothing. Any red-blooded male given *carte blanche* to kiss her, and in such provocative circumstances, might have been similarly affected. She ought to be grateful that he hadn't taken advantage of the situation. If he had, goodness only knew to what lengths her desire for him might have taken them. Now, there *would* have been cause for tears and regret.

Thus, sternly in control of herself, she was able to make a joke of her encounter with the scorpion.

'I feel quite mortified now,' she concluded lightly, 'behaving like some Victorian miss with a fit of the vapours.'

Throughout dinner she chatted determinedly to Lena of trivial matters, sedulously avoiding Dimitri's eye. And when the meal was over she remained at Lena's side until host and hostess showed signs of retiring, when she rose too, and with a hurried general goodnight made for the security of her bedroom.

But she was not ready for sleep and her room was warm. She threw open the long windows that gave on to a balcony circling the house, then went into the en suite bathroom, where she showered and washed her hair.

When she returned to the bedroom it was not appreciably cooler and, clad only in the flimsiest of nighties, she sat down at the dressing-table to dry and then to brush the almost living texture of her red-gold hair.

The dressing-table mirror reflected the windows, and Chryssanti was suddenly aware of movement behind the curtains partially obscuring them. It was ridiculous of course on this uninhabited island, but her first thought was of burglars and she swung round in alarm, her lips parted, ready to scream.

The sound was stillborn as she recognised the intruder. But, instead of stilling her fears, recognition increased the palpitations of her heart.

'You . . . you gave me such a fright.'

'I'm sorry,' Dimitri said as he stepped further into the room and closed the curtains behind him.

'Wh-what are you doing here? What do you want?'

He came closer and stood looking down at her, his handsome features grave, his dark eyes unfathomable. His expression gave nothing away, but as he continued his silent appraisal Chryssanti felt that hers was an open book.

CHAPTER EIGHT

DIMITRI stretched out a hand towards her and lifted a strand of the still slightly damp hair. Slowly he wound the red-gold tress around his finger, his eyes seemingly intent on his actions.

Chryssanti found she was holding her breath, and she let it go in a long sound of exasperation.

'Dimitri, for heaven's sake! I asked you what you want.'

He let his hand fall to his side.

'What do I want? Surely that must be obvious. I want to have that talk you have been avoiding all evening.'

She stared at him incredulously. 'You want to talk about me being scared by a scorpion?'

His eyes narrowed,

'Do not prevaricate, Chryssanti. We both know that was not the prime reason for your distress.'

'No.' she agreed quickly. 'I was hot and overtired. It was silly of me to think I could do without a siesta.'

He dismissed this as the fabrication it was. 'The heat, your fatigue, would both have been as nothing if you had been happy.'

'I had no reason to be unhappy.'

'No?' His expression was sardonic. 'Let us stop this fencing, Chryssanti. Let us at least be honest with each other.'

'I've been perfectly honest with you,' she retorted, 'all the time. Only you never seem to believe me.' She stood up suddenly, then wished she hadn't as the movement brought her perilously close to him, into the dangerous aura of his masculinity. 'Oh, Dimitri,' her voice shook a little, 'you're not on about this Christos business again, are you—not after we agreed...?'

'Indirectly, yes.'

'And just what does that mean?'

'It means,' he said with a note of ferocity in his voice, 'that ever since you realised you do not love my brother any more, you have been left with a gap in your life— a gap you seem to be attempting to fill.'

For a moment she looked at him uncomprehendingly. Then, gradually, the import of his words penetrated. She sat down again, hard, feeling suddenly sick.

'That... that's a rotten thing to say,' she whispered.

'Not if it's true. You're a young, impressionable girl...'

'I'd hardly call twenty-two *young*. And I'm a woman, not a child!'

'You may not be young in years,' he admitted. 'But I am willing to bet you are young in experience. Tell me, Chryssanti,' he said huskily, 'are you still a virgin?' And, as she stared at him in mute defiance, he said, 'Never mind! Your silence is answer enough.'

She swung round on the padded stool, turning her back on him, and began to play a restless, jerky game with the jars and bottles on the dressing-table top.

'All right!' she muttered savagely. 'So I've never slept with a man. What's it got to do with you? What's it got to do with anything? Is there something wrong with being a virgin?'

'Not at all. In this day and age, it is a cause for congratulation. But, as I said, it means you are lacking in experience. You are untouched, a little romantic perhaps, as befits your artistic nature. And a little curious about the ways of love?' He had moved to stand behind her so that she could see his reflection, close to hers, in the mirror. But even if the mirror had not been there she would have sensed his proximity. It was as though a glowing heat transmitted itself from him to her. The old man-to-woman alchemy, strong and inevitable.

'You are curious about love,' he repeated, 'and also perhaps a little "in love with love"? For a young woman to have a lover is a status symbol, *ne*?' As he spoke he had rested his hands on her shoulders, but Chryssanti wrenched herself free and slid from the stool, putting several feet of safety between them.

Angry now, fists clenched at her side she confronted him.

'That's what I'd call a typical male chauvinist attitude! Well, I can't really say I'm surprised to find it here in Greece. I've noticed that women still haven't quite attained equality. So having a man is a status symbol, is it? And what is it called when a man has a string of women friends? Just a few extra notches on his bedpost?'

His face darkened. 'That expression implies promiscuity. It is an insult!'

'It wasn't meant as such. OK, maybe you *are* as pure as the driven snow. I don't know, just as *you* don't know *my* attitude towards men. But, for your information, I've never wanted a man just so I could flaunt him to make my friends envious. I may not be as old as *you*, or as experienced, but neither am I that immature!'

'And that gap in your life that I spoke of?'

She had almost forgotten the earlier twists and turns of their conversation. She sank down on the side of the bed.

'All right,' she said more soberly. 'After all these years it *does* feel a little strange to realise that I don't love Christos. But in no way am I consciously looking for a replacement. If I meet someone, all well and good. I'm not denying I'd like to be married some day.'

'And what about your career?'

'I'd like to make use of my degree, but I don't think I'm a dedicated career-woman, not to the extent of making it my whole life.' And then she remembered the rest of his implication. 'And to imply that I've been trying to make use of *you*...' Her voice faltered away into silence. She hadn't been using him as he'd implied, but he certainly had filled that empty gap in her heart, filled it to overflowing.

For, after all, it hadn't been much of a void that Christos had left. Dimitri was twice the man his brother could ever be.

'What else am I to think,' he asked more gently, 'when you deliberately provoke my interest, invite my kisses?'

He was justified in that accusation at least, and Chryssanti flushed to the roots of her hair.

'I...I thought,' she choked on the words, 'I thought you *wanted* to kiss me. You...you *said* you did. Oh!' She buried her face in her hands. 'What is it with you, Dimitri Mavroleon? You can make me feel about an inch high.'

The side of the bed sagged under his weight as he lowered himself to sit beside her and his arm went about her shoulders.

'I do not mean to belittle you and I *did* want to kiss you, Chryssanti,' he said softly. 'I have always wanted to kiss you. But I wanted *you* to kiss *me* for the right reasons.' He pulled her hands from her face and tilted her chin up so that she had to meet his eyes.

'What...what sort of reason?' she asked shakily.

'No man worth his salt wants to feel he is a substitute for another, that he is merely filling a vacancy. I wanted you to kiss me because I am *myself*. That is why I rejected you in the cave. And that is why you wept. Not because of the scorpion, but because of my rejection, *ne*?'

It seemed to be a time for total honesty on both sides.

'Yes,' she whispered.

'So tell me, Chryssanti,' he persisted, 'why did you ask me to kiss you? The truth, please. I shall know if you lie to me.'

Her eyelids fluttered down and she shook her head, her teeth worrying at her full lower lip.

'Chryssanti!' he urged, and the pressure of his fingers on her chin increased.

'I...I can't tell you that. It's too embarrassing.'

'The truth should never embarrass. Look at me, Chryssanti, and tell me. Did you just want to be kissed by someone, by anyone, or...?'

'No.' She nerved herself to look at him and, caught by the expression in his dark eyes, found she could not look away again. 'It was *you* I wanted to kiss me.'

'Why?' His catechism was inexorable.

'Because...because...' But the truth was too stark, would make her too vulnerable. 'I...'

'All right!' He sounded amused. 'I will not press you any further for the moment. But I shall ask you again for the answer to that. And now...' He released her chin and let his hand slide up over her cheek, cupping her face in his warm palm while his fingers sensuously caressed the sensitive skin behind her ear. 'And what now?'

It was a conundrum to which she did not know the answer either.

'Perhaps,' she said diffidently, 'you ought to go now, now that you know...'

'But I know nothing yet, except the answer to one question. There are many others in my mind.'

'Couldn't we talk about those tomorrow?' She made a half-hearted attempt to free herself. Their faces were close, their bodies just touching as he held her still.

There was a moment of exquisite tension, a tension that stretched between them. Her nerves tautened and quivered, then he leaned towards her and brushed her lips with his own. It was a mothlike contact with no pressure. It did not linger half long enough for Chryssanti, and yet her entire body had begun to pulsate.

'These questions have no need of speech,' Dimitri murmured against her mouth. 'They can be easily answered here and now.' As he spoke, he turned her fully into his embrace.

Her mind urged resistance, but she was not listening as he kissed her again—and oh, such a different kiss. There was nothing tentative about it this time. It held a singing passion that aroused a sweet, sensuous ache within her ungiven body. There was no way she could hide her response and she clung frantically, returning him kiss for kiss, fiery desire scorching through her.

'Chryssanti, *agape mou*!' His voice was fierce yet tender as he said her name followed by a long string of words in his own language which she did not understand.

His hands moved hungrily over the silky flimsiness that covered her body, arousing her to fever pitch. And when, encountering no resistance, no protest from her, his hand slipped inside the V of her nightdress to capture a swelling breast, she felt the nipple spring to life against his palm.

'There is so much you have to learn of love, Chryssanti *mou*,' he murmured against her ear, his warm breath a further source of eroticism, 'and I want to be the one to teach you.'

That was what she wanted too, she thought hazily as gently he pressed her shoulders, lowering her backwards on to the bed. He followed her down until they lay full-length in each other's arms, one of his long, muscular legs holding her a willing prisoner.

She wished he were undressed too, so that she could know the feel of his warm, naked flesh on hers, and she began to struggle with the buttons of his shirt. One by one they gave way to her importunate fingers until she could feel the warmth of life beating under the smooth skin with its fine coating of coarse hair.

His hand touched her leg, brushing her nightdress back over her thigh in a slow, tantalising movement that made her breath catch in her throat, sensitising every nerve in her body. He continued his exploration as far as her hip, and then her soft buttocks knew his proprietorial caresses.

She trembled uncontrollably as his hand moved gently, gradually, expertly, tenderly insistent, making more intimate demands until it made an electrifying contact that caused a trembling awakening, making her arch against him with a little cry of pleasure.

'Dimitri, oh, Dimitri!' Her breath sobbed in her throat as, in the grip of a sudden frenzy of wanting, she said his name over and over again, oblivious to everything but the sensations he was causing.

He had wanted to teach her the secrets of love and he was succeeding, showing her her body's needs.

She wanted him to satisfy the passion his seductive fingers had ignited. She wanted that spark of feeling to erupt fully into ecstatic fulfilment. But she wanted to give him pleasure, too. She wanted him to take her, and she undulated against him with a wantonness she had never known she possessed. But as she moved her hands over him in a seeking caress, discovering his hard arousal, stirring her own loins still more, he made a little sound of negation and lifted himself away from her.

She sought to pull him back, murmuring a protest, but he was adamant.

'No, Chryssanti!' He sat on the edge of the bed, dark head bowed, his chest rising and falling as he sought to steady his breathing and running his hands through his already dishevelled hair.

His sudden withdrawal smote her like a pain and, her body registering its sense of deprivation, she curled foetus-like on the bed, hugging herself in an access of agony. A choked sob escaped her and at once he turned towards her, compunction in his face.

'I am sorry, Chryssanti *mou*. Forgive me. I had not intended things to go so far.' He reached out and touched her arm, 'But you are so sweet, so very lovely. . . so very feminine and desirable. And I am only human. If it is any consolation,' his sensual mouth curled in a sudden grimace that told her of his fight with his own agonising need, 'you are not alone in your suffering.'

'Then why. . .?' she began, but could not complete the question.

He sighed and again his hand tousled his hair.

'Because wanting is not enough, is it, Chryssanti *mou*? There is more to love than that.'

She flinched inwardly. He certainly couldn't have made it much clearer. He was telling her that he'd wanted her but he did not love her. She ought to be thankful, she supposed, for his integrity. But she wished he had never set out to teach her the needs of her body which would never be at rest again.

Only pride sustained her through the next few moments as he straightened himself and walked slowly towards the door. On the threshold, he paused and looked back at her. There was concern in his face and uncertainty in his eyes.

'You will be all right?' he asked.

Lips tightly set to stop her crying out a denial, to stop her begging him to stay, she nodded—and then he was gone and she could give way to her agonising pain of body and mind.

Chryssanti thought she understood Dimitri's attitude in the days that followed. Not even by implication did he make any reference to that impassioned scene in her bedroom, and she guessed he was wishing it had never happened. Even so, he seemed to go out of his way to keep his promise that she should enjoy every remaining moment of her stay on Helenos.

Sometimes alone, sometimes with Marcos and Lena, they walked, swam, discussed topics of mutual interest, occasionally arguing amicably over some difference of opinion. And she *did* enjoy herself, though not as much as she would have done had her heart not been so bruised and her body still hungry for Dimitri's lovemaking.

She painted, too, and by the end of their week on Helenos she felt she was beginning to understand and perhaps even to capture the essence of the Greek landscape and its dramatic qualities. For there *was* drama in the ever-present restless sea, carving its way into the rocky land. There was drama in the scattered stepping-stone islands vanishing towards the horizon in a sequence of perspectives of black, purple and blue.

She was sorry in one way when the time came to leave the lovely pagan peace of the island. But there was an all too insidious security in the way time seemed to be standing still, isolating the four of them in an idyllic existence. Despite her essentially romantic nature, Chryssanti was realistic enough to know that precious moments could not be held encapsulated. Life must move on. And she knew too that it was better that it should. Even though, when they returned to Skiapelos and from there inevitably to the mainland and Athens, she had a difficult decision to make.

She had two choices. She could accept Dimitri's offer of help to make herself a career in Athens. That way she could continue seeing him, in the hope that their now friendly relationship might deepen.

Or she might do better to accept that he wasn't in love with her and was never likely to be, cut her losses, return to England and try to forget him. The decision was postponed by other considerations.

During their absence from Skiapelos there had been new arrivals at Thalassios's villa—Anastasia, accompanied by Chryssanti's brother, Stephen Forster.

'Manoli flew Stephen and me over in the firm's helicopter,' Anastasia explained as she greeted her eldest son and his companions. 'He was bringing Stephen here anyway for the school holidays, so I thought it was too good an opportunity to miss.'

'How's Fortula?' Anxiously Lena put the question that was uppermost in Chryssanti's mind, and Chryssanti felt Dimitri look sharply at her.

'Much, much better, thank heaven. But she has to stay in hospital, probably until the child is born.'

'And Christos?' Dimitri asked with apparent casualness, but Chryssanti knew better.

'Very relieved. I have never seen your brother so distraught as he was when he arrived at the hospital. He is remaining in Athens, of course.'

It was a great relief to Chryssanti that she was able to feel pleasure for Christos and Fortula. Another happy ending. Everyone seemed to be having happy endings but herself, she reflected wryly.

The trend of her thoughts must have shown in her face.

'And what do *you* think about Fortula's recovery, Chryssanti?' Dimitri asked quietly.

'It's splendid news!' She looked him squarely in the face. 'I couldn't be more pleased.' Then, her tawny eyes earnest, she reached out an impulsive hand to touch his arm. 'Honestly, Dimitri! I *mean* it!'

'*Kala!* Good!' His smile was warmly approving. For an instant he covered her hand with his own, and she felt a brief glow of pleasure that ended all too soon. 'And now, I expect, you will be anxious to see your brother?'

'Yes, of course!' she exclaimed, feeling guilty that she could have forgotten. 'Tassia, where's Stephen?'

'With your grandfather. But wait, Chryssanti; before you go to look for him, there is some news for you— bad news, I'm afraid.'

'Bad news?' Dry-mouthed, she looked at the older woman and felt only faintly reassured when Dimitri moved closer. 'Not . . . not one of my grandparents? Not Nan and Gramps Forster?' she pleaded.

'No, no!' Anastasia set a reassuring hand on her arm. 'But your uncle Domenicos. The day before yesterday. A heart attack.'

'A heart attack? Was it a bad one? Is he . . . ?'

'I am afraid so.'

'Poor Uncle Dom!' Tears filled Chryssanti's eyes. 'He's always been so good to me, to all of us. There'll be arrangements to make. I . . .'

'It will all be taken care of, Chryssanti,' Tassia told her. 'As Domenicos had no living family besides you and his sister—and obviously Tina is too frail—Manoli has flown to England to make the funeral arrangements.'

'Where?' Chryssanti asked anxiously, remembering her uncle's nostalgia for his homeland.

'Do not worry! Domenicos is to be brought back to Athens for burial.'

'And then, I imagine,' Dimitri put in, 'you will be involved in a great deal of business transactions? As his heiress you are going to be a very wealthy young woman.' There was an odd note in Dimitri's voice, but when Chryssanti looked at him his expression was unfathomable.

Though Chryssanti was genuinely grieved to hear of her elderly uncle's death, the shock was cushioned somewhat by a greater relief that her beloved grand-parents were in good health. The notion of her own im-minent wealth and the ensuing responsibilities had not really sunk in and was the least of her considerations. Soberly she went to look for her brother.

The years between this meeting and the last had added to Stephen's stature, of course, but otherwise he was not substantially changed. He had always been of a quiet and placid nature. Now, she gathered, he was also nat-urally studious, and doing well at the school Thalassios had chosen for him.

He was a little shy with Chryssanti at first, but Dimitri's presence eased the tension. It was obvious that the admiration Stephen had originally conceived for his cousin had not lessened. And, somewhat wryly,

Chryssanti conceded that, four years ago, her young brother had shown more perception than she in his choice of an idol.

Since she was reunited with her brother, there was no question of her leaving Skiapelos immediately—except of course for the sad occasion of Domenicos's funeral.

This ceremony, which took place a few days later, was efficiently orchestrated by the Mavroleon cousins, and Chryssanti had very little to do except attend and be present at the reading of the will.

To her surprise, Domenicos's solicitor insisted that initially only Chryssanti should be made aware of its contents.

'And for the time being, *thespinis*, until you have had time to reach a decision about Kyrios Theodopoulos's wishes, I suggest you do not reveal them to the rest of your family—or,' more obliquely, 'to anyone else who may have an interest.'

Though Chryssanti had already been aware of Domenicos's main intentions towards her, the actual details of his stipulations came as rather a surprise. But there would be certain legal and administrative formalities before her inheritance was made over to her, which gave her plenty of time to mull things over.

Naturally the Mavroleons showed their curiosity, but in different ways.

Lena and Marcos contented themselves with congratulating Chryssanti on her good fortune.

'And I'm so sorry about Domenicos,' Lena added soberly. 'He was a good man and a good boss.'

Tina was piqued that she was not immediately to know the terms of her late brother's will.

'Just give me a few days,' Chryssanti pleaded with her grandmother. 'There's a lot to think about and then I'll tell you everything, I promise.'

'What will you do about the Theodopoulos companies, in London and in Athens?' Dimitri asked her. *His* interest seemed coldly, formally polite, which added to her uncertainty. 'I assume you know nothing about oil and shipping? Will you sell out or will you appoint someone to run things for you?'

'I certainly shan't sell out. But it's an enormous responsibility—all that money. I don't think it's really sunk in yet.'

'I'm sure Marcos or our grandfather would be only too willing to advise you.'

'Marcos? My grandfather? But not *you*?' She looked at him searchingly.

'No!' The negative was delivered in a curt tone of voice that made her wonder even more. Since their return to Skiapelos there had been a diminution of his friendly manner.

Chryssanti had still not come to any firm conclusions when Thalassios Mavroleon sent for her. Despite his promise—or had it been more of a threat? she wondered wryly—she had seen very little of her grandfather during this visit. Now she had no doubt that he was going to do his own probing into her financial affairs. And she doubted that his approach would be subtle or that he would take kindly to any refusal to discuss her legacy. So it was with some trepidation that she made her way to the wing which held his and Tina's suite of rooms.

Her grandmother was not present.

'I am told that you are a painter?' Thalassios surprised her by saying without any preliminaries. 'That you want to paint my portrait?' Dimitri, of course. He

was the only one to whom she confided that ambition.
'Are you any good?'

'So I've been told,' Chryssanti said quietly. She
guessed Thalassios would hold no brief for false modesty.

'If it *is* any good, it will hang in the boardroom, at
the Corporation offices in Athens,' Thalassios told her.
'It is time to begin a new tradition. When I am gone,
you can paint Marcos.'

Chryssanti looked at him intently, but he didn't look
substantially frailer than usual, and she murmured the
expected conventionalities, which he received with
brusque matter-of-factness.

'You have nothing to gain by *my* death, at any rate.
When can you start?'

'Tomorrow? Now, if you like?'

'Tomorrow will do,' the old autocrat told her.

Thalassios made a splendid subject, as of course she'd
known he would. The snow-white thatch of hair, the dark
eyes still capable of fire, the haughty nose, the ageing
flesh drawn tightly over splendid bones, all gave im-
mense character to the portrait.

She had wondered if—with the restless energy of his
race—he would be able to sit still long enough. But he
gave her no cause for complaint on that score. Though
at the end of each session he insisted on seeing the pro-
gress of her work, for the first few sittings there was
little or no conversation and she was able to concentrate
on her task.

But as time went on he began to talk to her. At first
he spoke of family matters or of Greece's history. But
after a while she realised that, with more subtlety than
she'd given him credit for, he was quizzing her, finding

out more about her, about her likes and dislikes. He pooh-poohed the idea of a career.

'Your blood might be mixed, but you are a daughter of Greece, of Skiapelos. The women of my family marry and give their husbands sons to carry on our race.'

'I'm not saying I *shan't* get married—some day,' she defended herself. 'It's just that . . .'

'Children should be borne while a woman is young. You should marry now—and marry a Greek.'

'Why?' she bridled. 'What's wrong with Englishmen?' She had never forgotten and still found it hard to forgive Thalassios Mavroleon's denigration of her father.

'For an English *woman*, nothing!' His reply was almost placatory. 'But for you, who are half-Greek . . .' He spread his hands in a graceful, expressive gesture. 'You should marry Dimitri.'

Chryssanti swore, something she rarely did, as her hand jerked and marred a brushstroke, and Thalassios frowned in displeasure.

'I have spoken to Dimitri, and I believe he would be willing to have you.'

Chryssanti gave up all pretence of painting and stared at her grandfather.

'Whatever gives you that idea?'

His reply was an oblique one. 'You have recently become a very wealthy young woman. You are not accustomed to wealth. You will need someone to guide you. Who more suitable than a husband?'

Chryssanti felt sick suddenly, and her tongue clove to the roof of her mouth as she said bitterly, 'You mean Dimitri would be willing to marry me *for my money*?'

CHAPTER NINE

THALASSIOS seemed unmoved by her outburst.

'Why not?' he asked with an enquiring lift of his shaggy brows. 'His brothers, Christos and Manoli, have both taken wives from wealthy families. It is quite customary among we Greeks to ally fortune to fortune, business to business.'

'Business being the operative word,' Chryssanti said scornfully. 'They're business mergers, not marriages! That might have been true in Christos's case originally. But Manoli and Marianthe were very much in love. So were Marcos and Lena.' She stood up and began to pace the spacious apartment. Thalassios's words had unsettled her. She would achieve no more useful work today. To be married for what she possessed materially, not for personal reasons. How distasteful!

'Financial security is a very good basis for marriage,' her grandfather told her. 'It is fortunate for Marcos that he is my heir, for Helena brought him no dowry.'

'And you really think that would have mattered to Marcos?' Chryssanti was incredulous. 'You think if he hadn't been rich already he wouldn't have married her?'

'He would have been a fool!' the old man asserted.

'Better to be loved by a fool,' she exclaimed with feeling, 'than desired for mercenary reasons.'

'Sentimental claptrap!' Thalassios told her fiercely.

'Oh?' She began to clean her brushes. 'From what I hear,' she went on tartly, 'even you were in love once.' She regretted her words immediately as an expression of pain crossed her grandfather's face. 'Sorry,' she muttered, 'that was a bit below the belt. But anyway, I don't believe it of Marcos. You've only got to look at him to see how much he adores Lena. I think he'd have married her anyway.'

But what about Dimitri? Did she believe it of him? Unwittingly her grandfather echoed her thoughts.

'And what about Dimitri? Will you marry him if he asks you?'

'Not if he's after my money!' she retorted, unaware that, to the shrewd old man, her remark was a revealing one. 'Perhaps you don't understand English women, grandfather, and I *am* half-English, whether you like it or not. There may be the odd exception, but generally we don't go in for marriage for business purposes. And I want to be loved for myself. As my mother was,' she concluded defiantly. She didn't care if he was annoyed by the reference.

'And you are as headstrong and wilful as your mother!' Thalassios growled.

'And I hope that some day I'll be as happy as she was,' Chryssanti told him. With a decisive movement she thrust the clean brushes upright into a jar and made for the door.

'Where are you going?' Thalassios demanded. 'My sitting is not over.'

'It is for today,' she informed him sharply. 'I have to be in the right frame of mind to paint. The way I feel right now, I might just give you a pair of horns.'

To her surprise, as she quitted the apartment, she heard her grandfather give a short bark of laughter.

'You may be a sentimental fool, Granddaughter,' he shouted after her, 'but you have spirit. I will give you that.'

*   *   *

Chryssanti left one scene of conflict only to enter another. She might have spirit in one sense, as Thalassios had said, but in another sense her spirits were exceedingly low. Still depressed by her grandfather's implication that Dimitri was interested in her for her fortune, she had planned to walk in the grounds, perhaps even make her way to the Garden of the Gods, the ambience of which she always found soothing and uplifting.

But the sound of angry voices drew her instead to the villa's wide entrance hall, where Dimitri and Christos faced each other, with their mother an agitated onlooker. Chryssanti moved to her side.

'Tassia? Whatever's going on?' she asked in a low voice. But Anastasia wasn't given a chance to answer. Her niece's presence had been noted by both men.

'Chryssanti!' Christos's eyes lit up and he broke away from his brother, shouldering him aside and strode towards her. 'I have come here particularly to see you.'

'Oh?' Her heart sank and she cast an uneasy glance towards Dimitri. His classical features were set in grim lines.

'But this brother of mine is being more than usually obstructive,' Christos complained.

'I . . . I really can't think why you should want to see *me*,' Chryssanti told him.

'Oh, as usual he has a very plausible excuse,' Dimitri put in sarcastically. 'But it is one I do not credit for a moment. He says he is here to take you back to Athens, to . . .'

'What?' For a moment her imagination ran riot.

'I *told* Dimitri! It has to do with the Theodopoulos Company,' Christos explained irritably. 'They want you to come over to the mainland for a few days—on business. It is about time my grandfather joined the present century! With no telephones on Skiapelos, I had to fly over to give you the message myself.' Each of the Mavroleons had his own private helicopter.

'Why you?' Dimitri demanded.

'I was just about to explain that, only you gave me no opportunity. Manoli is in Paris on Mavroleon business.' He turned his back on his brother. 'Chryssanti, it seems there are more legal documents for you to sign and the lawyers want to know what you plan to do about..."the special conditions"?' He looked at her enquiringly. 'Do you know what...?'

'Yes, I understand,' Chryssanti interrupted him hastily. Those 'special conditions' had been very much in her thoughts in the last few moments. She was conscious of enormous relief that Christos's motives seemed to be quite above board. She turned to his brother. 'I was expecting this, Dimitri. I'll have to go back to Athens with him.'

'Then I shall accompany you.' His expression was still austere.

'I don't need anyone to go with me. You can't, anyway. My business is...is confidential.' Still bristling from her conversation with Thalassios, Chryssanti thought she saw Dimitri's motives.

'Damn your confidential business!' It was a long time since she'd heard Dimitri speak so angrily. 'I am not interested in your financial affairs.' If only she could believe that! 'I shall be accompanying you solely for the sake of propriety. You will not fly to Athens alone with Christos.'

'*Theos mou!*' Christos swore. 'Are you still riding that old hobby-horse?'

'Yes,' Dimitri said flatly. 'For I still do not trust you, little brother. And until Fortula is well enough to protect her own interests, I shall continue to do so.'

Cynically, Chryssanti found herself wondering just how much Fortula's interests still concerned Dimitri. Wasn't it more likely, she wondered, that—despite his denial—he was determined to keep *her*, Chryssanti, in sight for reasons of his own—reasons that concerned her newly acquired fortune?

The helicopter took off, and with a feeling of sadness Chryssanti watched the little cluster of islands fall away below and behind them. She would be returning in a day or two, but it might be for a very short duration. In those few days she must make the decision whether or not to return to England.

Because of the noise of the rotating blades, conversation was almost impossible. But Christos seemed determined to talk to her despite Dimitri's presence close beside her.

'Shall you stay in Athens and run your uncle's company?' he shouted.

'I know nothing about it. I shall leave the running of the business to my uncle's manager, Costas. He seems very capable, and I know my uncle trusted him implicitly. He was with Uncle Dom for years.'

'But you, what will you do?' Christos pressed.

Did she feel Dimitri tense as the brothers waited for her reply?

'On the whole,' she said slowly, 'I think it would be better if I went back to England.'

'Why?' It was Dimitri who asked the abrupt question.

'That's obvious, isn't it?' Christos mocked. 'She's got a boyfriend there, remember? Terry. How else was she able to resist *my* fatal charms?' Chryssanti knew he was joking, but she sensed Dimitri's anger. 'And I'm quite sure *he'll* be waiting faithfully for *her*,' Christos went on. 'What man would risk losing such a wealthy wife?'

They arrived in Athens too late to visit the lawyers' offices that day. Christos was most pressing in his invitation that Chryssanti and Dimitri should spend the night at his town house. Chryssanti would have refused anyway, but to her indignation she wasn't given the chance.

'You forget,' Dimitri told his brother, 'Chryssanti has her own accommodation in Athens now.'

She had, of course. Four years ago, when Lena had first brought her and her brother to Athens, Chryssanti had stayed briefly in the penthouse suite which formed part of the apartment building belonging to Domenicos Theodopoulos and which was now her property.

'Where will *you* stay?' she asked Dimitri. The limousine which had brought them from the airport had deposited an aggrieved Christos at his own front door and was now drawing up outside the Theodopoulos building.

'I assume your apartment boasts a spare bedroom?' Dimitri asked drily as he followed her from the vehicle.

'Several. But...but you surely don't expect to stay here...with me...alone?'

'Naturally!'

Her reaction was a mixture of indignation and an unwilling, quivering excitement. How, she wondered, would Dimitri go about proposing to her? For if—as Thalassios believed—Dimitri *did* plan to propose, this might be his way of creating an undisturbed opportunity.

If it hadn't been for her wretched inheritance, how she would have welcomed such a proposal. Instead she dreaded it. She must turn down the one thing she desired above all else. For there was no way she would accept an offer made for financial reasons. He mustn't be given the chance, not here, not now. She wasn't ready to face it.

'You can't stay,' she told him.

He ignored her words, put a firm hand at her elbow and steered her into the building. A quiet explanation from him to the concierge obtained a key, the Mavroleon name as always a sure passport. Chryssanti doubted if there were anyone in Athens who did not know the name and jump to attention at the sound of it.

'I shall be staying with you for your protection,' Dimitri said as they entered the lift.

'Protection!' she exclaimed. 'From what or whom?' Because Thalassios's insinuations were still rankling, she went on somewhat rashly, 'It seems to me I'm more in need of protection from *you*!'

Immediately she could have bitten her tongue out. She hadn't meant to reveal her suspicions of him. At least, not yet. She'd decided that Dimitri was going to get a shock if and when he did propose.

But she need not have worried. He misunderstood. His features were glacial.

'You need not concern yourself. If I had been going to take advantage of you, I had plenty of opportunity, both on Skiapelos and on Helenos. And as I recall, *I* was the one who exercised restraint—on more than one occasion!'

They had reached the penthouse floor. Her cheeks flaming with humiliation, Chryssanti stumbled out of the lift. At the door of her suite she made one more attempt to outface him.

'If protection is all you have in mind, you've done your duty. You've seen me to my front door. I'll be perfectly all right now.' Stiffly, 'I'd rather you didn't stay.'

But he had the key.

'I am staying,' he repeated brusquely as he unlocked the door.

'It's not as if you've nowhere to go,' she argued as he urged her across the threshold. 'Christos would put you up.'

He closed the apartment door behind him with an air of finality.

'You need not fear I shall inflict even my company on you,' he went on curtly. 'You need not see me until morning—unless you yourself wish it.'

'Which I shan't!' she snapped.

He inclined his head in acceptance of her dictum. 'Which room may I use?'

With a shrug she indicated her complete indifference. In truth, she could not trust herself to speak. It was going to be torture being completely alone under the same roof as Dimitri. Together, yet because of her knowledge they could not be more divided.

In the bedroom she had chosen for herself she looked around her. The luxuriously furnished penthouse suite was in pristine condition. She guessed that it was always kept that way in readiness for the owner's use. It was still difficult to think of herself as the owner. And already she was experiencing some the problems that wealth could bring.

The large double bed looked invitingly comfortable. But to Chryssanti it cried out to be occupied by two people. With an impatient mutter at her own foolish thoughts, she unpacked the small suitcase she'd brought, laid out her nightdress and négligé, then moved into the adjoining bathroom to shower.

It was going to be a sultry night, as sultry as her thoughts. Already she felt hot and sticky, and she let the water run cool.

As she showered, she wondered what Dimitri was doing right at this moment. Was he showering, too? She shuddered involuntarily, closing her eyes as all too easily her imagination conjured up the picture of his bronzed naked body, the play of strong muscles beneath the silky satin of his skin.

From there it was only a short step to imagining him here with her, sharing *her* shower. Easy to picture how it would be. Soaping each other's bodies, lingering over the more intimate areas, until touch became arousing caresses. Moist kisses, deepening, intensifying. A suddenly impatient Dimitri sweeping her up in his arms, carrying her, still damp, through to the bedroom, making love to her, awakening her senses until finally...

Her eyes snapped open. Stop it, stop it, she adjured herself angrily. The situation was bad enough without these inflammatory imaginings. Her body was aching nearly as much as if Dimitri *were* here with her.

With a quick movement she turned the controls until the water ran icy cold, making her gasp. Then she snatched up a towel and dried herself with almost brutal briskness, concentrating her thoughts on tomorrow's interview with Domenicos Theodopoulos's lawyers.

But as she stepped from the shower cabinet she caught a glimpse of herself in the full-length mirror and paused to study her appearance.

Long, lightly tanned limbs. Full but firmly jutting breasts. Narrow waist flaring out into gently rounded hips. She turned from side to side, smoothing her hands down over her slim flanks.

Chryssanti had never suffered from vanity. Until recently she had taken her body and its feminine attributes for granted. Now she was unable to resist studying herself, wondering how a man would see her naked shapeliness. No, not just any man, but how *Dimitri* would see her. Whether he would like what he saw.

Again she had to force her mind back to reality. Dimitri had already proved that he found her physically attractive. But in all their encounters he'd never once mentioned the word love. And if he were to mention it now, after what his grandfather had said, she would suspect him of hypocrisy.

In the bedroom once more she pulled on her nightdress and moved to open the french windows. The night air of Athens might not be as sweet or pure as that on Skiapelos, but she knew she would feel stifled with them closed.

Her room overlooked the rooftop terrace, a substitute garden adorned with statuary and flowering shrubs. There was a full moon riding over the city and, drawn by an irresistible impulse, Chryssanti stepped out into the coolly lit area. She leaned her elbows on the stone balcony rail and stared out dreamily over sleeping Athens.

High above it, like the prow of some insubstantial and ghostly ancient ship, rode the floodlit classic lines of the Acropolis. She gazed wistfully at it. Memories of her visit there with Dimitri were unavoidable.

Unforgettable, too, were the comparisons he had made between her and the marble columns of the ancient citadel—in the morning 'as cool as your pearly skin', at sunset 'gold and red as if on fire, just like your hair'.

It seemed incredible that within the same man such a poetic nature could go hand in hand with the mercenary qualities she suspected.

'And at night,' she reminisced softly, unaware that she was speaking aloud, 'it has a truly mystical beauty.'

'You remember?'

With a stifled gasp Chryssanti spun round on her heel. She had not realised that the room Dimitri had chosen adjoined hers, that his window too looked out upon the terrace.

'You . . . you startled me,' she told him unnecessarily. Her pulses leapt erratically as her fascinated gaze took in the fact that he was clad only in a short, thigh-skimming robe. The hair clung damply to his thighs. His dark hair was damp, too. He *had* been showering at the same time as her, and, remembering her earlier torrid imaginings, she flushed hotly.

Dimitri moved closer, his dark eyes making their own intent appraisal.

'A truly mystical beauty,' he repeated her words. 'Yes, you do look very ethereal in the moonlight, especially so in that white gown. Like some goddess come down from Mount Olympus.'

Too late she recalled just how scantily she was clad. The flimsy nightdress clung silkily to her body, delineating every voluptuous curve. The transparent cups of the bodice could not conceal the fact that her nipples had hardened at the sight and sound of him. She folded her arms protectively.

'It . . . it's very hot, isn't it?' she babbled. 'I was just getting some fresh air before I go to bed.' She began to sidle towards her still open window, then came to an abrupt halt. He hadn't seemed to move, but somehow the way was blocked.

'Why go yet?' he asked. 'It is such a beautiful night. A night for looking at the stars.' But his eyes were fixed firmly on her flushed, aware face, the widened, darkened eyes, the slightly parted lips, which drew in the breath that gently agitated her breasts.

Just the nearness of his magnificent, barely covered body was enough to create nervous tension inside her. His male aura was as potent as if his arms were even now wrapped around her.

She swallowed nervously.

'Dimitri, I . . .'

'May I not stay here with you a while?' he coaxed. 'Could we not enjoy the night together?'

She gasped again, misunderstanding him.

'*What?*'

He gave an impatient, disclaiming gesture. 'I meant the stars, the moon, the view of the city.' But all the same he was very close to her now, only inches away, looking down into her eyes.

'You said I wouldn't see you again until the morning,' she reminded him, inwardly cursing the breathlessness that made her voice so unsteady, the reproof so uncertain.

'Is my company really so odious to you, Chryssanti *mou*?' he asked her gently. He reached out an exploratory hand and with one finger he traced the line of her temple, her jaw, the shape of her soft mouth, lingering on the full lower lip. She couldn't move. His touch seemed to leave a fiery trail of sensation. 'Chryssanti?' he said again on a questioning note, and she felt the muscles of her stomach contract wrenchingly.

His voice had that quality that she'd once heard described as 'dark brown'—husky, emotive. It pulled unbearably at her senses. He went on, his tone even more seductive.

'Recently I had begun to believe you enjoyed being with me. Has anything happened to change that?'

She couldn't very well tell him about her heated exchange with Thalassios, and so she remained silent. And he took her silence for encouragement.

'I am sorry if you thought my behaviour today a little high-handed,' he continued. 'But I meant it when I said I still do not trust Christos. I could not let you come to Athens alone with him. It would not be the first time he has philandered with another woman. And if I had left you here alone in the apartment, I could not be sure he would not visit you here.'

'And you still couldn't trust me to repel his advances?' The thought hurt.

'I do not know what to think.' He said it fiercely. 'All I know is that the thought of you in his arms...' He did not complete his sentence, but his lips were grimly drawn and at his sides his hands were bunched into fists.

It was almost as if he were jealous, Chryssanti thought, staring at him wonderingly. But jealousy would presuppose the presence of some other similarly strong emotion.

As he continued to stare into her eyes, her heart hammered in her throat. His gaze was hypnotic, and she had to exert tremendous will-power to prevent herself swaying towards him. It was as if an inexorable force was pulling them together, a sexual aura so palpable that it could almost be seen and touched. Did he feel it too?

It seemed he did, for suddenly, before she could realise his purpose, he reached out for her, gathered her into his arms. She knew the steely hard pressure of his magnificent body against hers. The heightened sound, the increased rapidity of his breathing, the intensity with which he held her made her tremble.

'Dimitri! Please! I...'

'Don't fight me, Chryssanti *mou*,' he pleaded with her. Then, before she could say another word, he had pressed his warm lips against hers and was kissing her with a combination of urgency and delicacy that destroyed all coherent thought, any intentions she might have had of fighting him off.

Lost in the warm, sensuous pull of his masculinity, deep inside she felt insatiable longing begin to surge, and as she parted her lips to the exploration of his their breath mingled, becoming one long sigh of mutual arousal.

With the submission of her mouth to his there came the thrusting invasion of his tongue, parodying deeper intimacies, the kiss soon taking on a barbaric, compelling sexuality that made her cling blindly to his broad shoulders, as every fibre of her being shuddered its response.

He was not immune to the sensual vibrations running through her, and as his hands began their feverish glissade over her silken-clad figure she was deliciously aware how little separated her flesh from his.

She gave into the longing of her hands to explore his body. Beneath the towelling robe his chest hair was excitingly rough to her palms. With her fingertips she commenced a circular massage of the male nipple, heard the breath catch in his throat and knew just what the hardening of his thighs presaged.

His loosely belted robe had fallen open, releasing his rising male hardness to surge against her, and she dared to touch him. She wanted him to touch her too, as he had that night in her room, at the villa on Helenos,

wanted him to elicit those same sensations that had come
so tantalisingly close to satisfaction.

At the gentle enclosure and pressure of her fingers he
gave a sudden exclamation that was almost a groan. For
a moment he thrust the pulsating hardness of his masculinity against her. Then he swept her up into his arms,
and with his mouth still on hers carried her over the
threshold into her room.

As he slid the nightdress from her shoulders, his whole
body was taut with an urgency she shared.

Her mind clouded by the desires of her body, her dark
suspicions were forgotten. She only knew that she loved
this man and that she wanted the hungry, mindless
abandon of passion shared and fulfilled.

They were both naked now, standing breast to breast,
thigh to thigh. His deep shudders told her of her effect
on him. Lower and lower his hands moved, sealing her
against him for the full length of their bodies, making
her quiveringly aware of the full force of his manhood,
the strength of its primitive desires.

Her fingers raked the strong muscles of his back and
her head fell back, exposing the long column of her neck
to his mouth. She arched her body towards him in a
gesture of total surrender.

'Oh, Dimitri!' The name was an anguished gasp
against his lips. 'Please, please...' She could stand the
torture no longer. She wanted him to take her now, to
make love to her fully.

Gently he lowered her on to the bed and knelt over
her. Her excitement grew. Soon she would know his
possession.

But he seemed in no hurry now that his objective was
in sight. Tentatively, questingly, he touched her, his lips
following his hand over her body, lifting, caressing each

breast, his head bent to kiss each one, to tease each hard, erect nipple. Sensually he caressed her smooth stomach.

At the tormenting delay she gave an inarticulate cry, as revealing of her need as if she had spoken it.

Then, as he had done once before, his hands sought and found the evocative secret places that aroused her.

Her muscles ached from straining to meet him and at last he took pity on her, entering her, moving rhythmically, and at last she knew the glorious perfection of feeling her flesh fused with his.

His lovemaking was powerful but skilful, taking not only his own pleasure and release but bringing her to the height of a physical ecstasy far greater than she had ever dreamed possible.

At last, lax in lazy contentment, they lay in each other's arms, and Chryssanti was almost on the verge of sleep when she heard him murmur, 'You will not go back to England now!'

The complacency of his tone jerked her back to full awareness. 'Why? What do you mean?'

'I mean that you will not marry your Terry now.'

Her thoughtless, reckless behaviour during the past half-hour brought home to her, Chryssanti sat up and looked down at him.

'Oh?' Then, her voice carefully expressionless, she asked, 'What makes you say that?'

'Because you'll have to marry *me* now.'

Still she held on to her cool neutrality. 'I don't see that necessarily follows.'

'You do not?' It was his turn to sit up.

'No!'

'Chryssanti, I am shocked!' He sounded more than shocked. He sounded piqued, angry. 'I had not expected you to allow me to make love to you unless you... I thought it was understood that we should marry.'

'Understood?' She seized on what seemed to be the operative word. 'Understood by whom? By Grandfather Thalassios? By you? But certainly not by me!'

'What has this to do with our grandfather?' She could almost have believed in the genuineness of his surprise if she hadn't known...

'Only that I'm grateful to him for the warning. Though I don't think he meant it as such.' She bounced off the bed and pulled her wrap around her, even though it afforded no more protection than her nightdress. 'But I'll tell you what I told *him*,' she went on. 'I don't want a marriage based on a business merger. I think the whole idea is despicable. I know Uncle Dom's money has suddenly made me a very desirable property. Well, if anyone thinks they're going to marry me for that, they've got a considerable shock coming to them.'

'I see!' As she spoke, Dimitri's face had grown colder and colder. Now he too stood up and donned his robe. His voice was as icy as his expression. 'You have made your feelings and opinions very clear. To think that I believed I had risen in your estimation!' His short bark of laughter was without humour. Savagely he jerked the belt of his robe into a knot. 'Well, this has taught me a lesson, Chryssanti. You need not fear any repetition of my proposal.' He moved towards the windows by which they'd entered.

'Proposal?' she jeered. 'The only kind of proposal I'd consider is one made out of love. I certainly wasn't aware that *you'd* made one. It sounded to me like an assumption—a totally unwarranted one.'

He was white and drawn around the mouth as he paused on the threshold to deliver his parting shot.

'Are you sure you *know* what love is, Chryssanti? I believe that *I* do. I had thought that *you* might love *me*. I hope for your sake you do not discover that you do, for I shall never ask for your love again.'

CHAPTER TEN

As HIS taut, erect figure disappeared through the french windows, the tears she had held back until now began to flow down Chryssanti's face and she felt the dawnings of a horrible doubt.

Dimitri's anger had sounded so genuine. Was it possible she had misjudged him? It wasn't until something like this happened that you realised just how little you knew a person.

Her doubt grew as she considered how slight was the evidence on which her suspicions had been based—a few words from her grandfather. She knew Dimitri better than she knew Thalassios Mavroleon.

Now Chryssanti was remembering other words that had been spoken about Dimitri. 'He has *philotimo*,' Marianthe had said. 'It means pride, self-respect, honesty.'

And Lena. She had said, 'Apart from Marcos, of course, I always think Dimitri's the nicest, the kindest of the Mavroleon men.' And Lena had been married to a Mavroleon for four years. How she wished Lena were here now to advise her, she thought as she crawled miserably into bed. Oh, such a different bed, now that it knew its occupant's heartache instead of physical rapture.

Her anguished thoughts kept her awake throughout most of the night. How she wished Domenicos had never made her his heir. Then there would never have been any question in her mind as to whether she was desired for herself. And now that she'd known Dimitri's lovemaking she could almost wish she'd been able to lower her pride, to marry him whatever his motive.

Her last conscious thought, just before she fell into an uneasy doze, was that at least she knew now what she must do tomorrow, what she must tell the lawyers.

Chryssanti's appointment was an early one. But, even so, she found Dimitri breakfasting before her. She had been dreading this encounter, afraid that she might find herself entirely unable to meet his eyes.

She need not have worried. He did not even glance her way, and his only answer to her nervous 'Good morning,' was an incomprehensible grunt.

She found after all that she could not face food. She downed a cup of coffee, snatched up her handbag and made for the door of the kitchenette.

'Will your business be concluded today?' His sudden question made her jump and she turned to face him.

'I think so.'

'Good. Then we will return to Skiapelos tonight. I imagine you have no wish to spend another night here?'

'N-no.'

That seemed to be the end of the conversation, but Chryssanti lingered in the doorway. This atmosphere of animosity was heartbreaking when she considered the rapport that had grown between them recently. Though her temper was quick, as fiery as her hair, Chryssanti had never been one to bear grudges for long. In a quarrel of any kind she was generally the first to apologise. And there was still this terrible uncertainty as to whether she had misjudged Dimitri Mavroleon.

She swallowed and moved back into the room.

'Dimitri...' Her voice trailed away as inimical dark eyes met hers, and she had to nerve herself all over again to go on. 'I—I just wanted to say...about last night...I...'

'Last night is a closed subject!' he snapped. 'It is finished. It never happened.' He waited, his eyes still holding hers, waited for her to dare to deny it.

She did not dare. Afraid that she might burst into tears again, she turned sharply on her heel and left the apartment.

Her business with the lawyers was soon concluded: a few signatures on imposing-looking documents after they had been explained to her.

'All that remains, *thespinis*,' the lawyer told her, 'is for you to give me your agreement to the special conditions set out in Kyrios Theodopoulos's will. Perhaps you would like to read them again?'

'No.' Even if Chryssanti hadn't been possessed of a retentive memory, the words would have been etched in her mind because of their association with the problem of Dimitri.

Domenicos had made his will four years ago, shortly after his reconciliation with Thalassios Mavroleon.

'I am an old man,' he had written, 'and I am ashamed that it has taken me so long to recognise the evils of money. Consequently I wish mine to be put to uses that will not bring unhappiness.

'I am not slighting my nephew Stephen Mavroleon in making his sister Chryssanti my sole heir. He will be provided for by his Mavroleon relations.

'But I do not wish my niece to find her inheritance a burden. As a rich woman, she might well be the prey of unscrupulous fortune-hunters. My wealth, therefore, is left to her conditionally.

'For as long as she remains single, it is hers to administer and use as she pleases. But on the day that she marries, three-quarters of her inheritance is to be divided among the following...' And here Domenicos had listed numerous charities.

'Do you wish to contest this clause, *thespinis*?' The lawyer had been patiently waiting for her attention to return to him.

'No,' Chryssanti sighed a little. 'I think it's a very sensible one.'

'Then all I have to ask is if you have any plans to marry in the foreseeable future?'

She shook her head.

'No. I wish I had.'

The lawyer unbent as far as his dry, professional manner would allow him.

'*Thespinis*, you are still young. I am sure that very soon I shall be hearing from you on this subject.'

Chryssanti wished she shared his confidence.

The flight back to Skiapelos was made in almost total silence. Chryssanti would have been grateful even for Christos's presence to break up the brooding atmosphere.

As they approached the island, below them she could see the *Poseidon* still riding at anchor in the hyacinth-blue waters of the man-made harbour. And a helicopter stood on the landing site adjacent to the villa.

'Christos, here again?' Chryssanti said in surprise as she stepped on to the tarmac.

'Manoli!' Dimitri said shortly. And, at her enquiring look, 'I recognise the registration number.'

'Of course. How silly of me.'

'Silly?' His tone was ironic. 'Perhaps it was wishful thinking? Perhaps you would have preferred it to be

Christos?' Oh, no, he wasn't starting *that* again! 'Since
it seems there was no emotion in your giving of yourself
to me, perhaps *he* would have served equally well.'

'Damn you! Oh, damn you!'

Chryssanti had never sworn at anyone in her life, much
less hit them. And now she stared in dismay at the red
imprints her fingers had left on Dimitri's swarthy cheek.

His hand shot out and for a hideous moment she
thought he too meant to strike. She had heard that, if
pushed too far, a Greek's quick temper could lead him
to violence. But instead Dimitri gripped her upper arm,
his fingers a painful vice.

'You will apologise for that!' he told her grimly.

Though she was close to tears again, Chryssanti ele-
vated her chin in a defiant gesture.

'Not until *you* apologise for your disgusting
suggestion.'

The heat pressed down like a lid as, eyes locked, they
glared at each other. Two proud people, each unwilling
to make the first move.

Chryssanti was the first to look away, but only because she knew she could hold back the threatening tears
no longer. With a choking sob she wrenched herself free,
turned and fled towards the villa.

'Chryssanti?' Lena met her at the entrance to the villa.
'I heard the "chopper".' Then she caught sight of the
younger girl's face. 'Good heavens! Whatever's the
matter? Have you had some more bad news?'

Lena was blocking the doorway and Chryssanti pushed
past her.

'Let me in before Dimitri catches up with me, please!'
she begged.

'You mean it's Dimitri who's upset you?' Lena hurried
after her as she made for her rooms.

'Who else? He's an expert at it!' Chryssanti slumped down on the side of her bed and blew her nose.

'What did he do? What did he say?'

'Oh, Lena, it's a long story. And it all seems so...so sordid.'

'Sordid?' Lena's face had paled. 'What did he *do*? He didn't...didn't...?'

'Oh, he didn't do anything I didn't *want* him to do,' Chryssanti confessed wearily. 'That part of it was as much my fault as his.'

'You *slept* together?'

'Well, that's the polite euphemism for it. We didn't actually *sleep*. When it was all over we had a flaming row and he walked out.'

Lena sat down beside Chryssanti. 'Do you want to talk about it? The row, I mean? What was it about?'

'Money! These damned Greeks and their love of money!' Chryssanti said explosively. 'I wish Uncle Dom had died a pauper.'

'Let's get this straight,' Lena said. 'You and Dimitri quarrelled over Domenicos's money?'

'Right!'

'Hmm, I see,' Lena said thoughtfully. She got up and began to pace around the room. 'I can see Dimitri's point.'

'You *can*?' Chryssanti was horrified. Surely four years of marriage to a Greek hadn't changed her friend that much, made *her* mercenary.

'Yes, Dimitri's a very proud man. He wouldn't like the idea of his wife being richer than he is. He wanted you to refuse your inheritance, I suppose?'

'*What?*' Chryssanti was beginning to wonder if she was going crazy, or if Lena was.

'He told me once,' Lena went on, 'just how much he admired Marcos for standing up to his grandfather, for refusing to marry Marianthe for her money. He said he'd never marry a woman he didn't love, either, that he wouldn't be pushed into one of Grandfather Thalassios's "mergers".'

Chryssanti suddenly realised that she was gaping like a stranded fish. She closed her mouth. Then opened it again to say faintly, 'Lena, I think I may have made the biggest mistake of my life. Listen!'

Swiftly she related the gist of her conversation with Thalassios Mavroleon and the accusations she had flung at Dimitri. As Chryssanti spoke, Lena looked more and more appalled.

'He asked you to marry him—and you said *that*? Oh, Chryssanti! And *are* you in love with him?'

Miserably Chryssanti nodded.

'You'll have to apologise to him.'

'Oh, but Lena, I...'

'If you want him, it's the only way. I like Greek men. But I know just how proud they are—so proud they will refuse to admit they are wrong. They have a tendency to dramatise the smallest incident into high tragedy. The Mavroleons are no exception. You know what their name means? Black Lion?' And, as Chryssanti nodded, 'Well, when they lose their temper they're as proud as any lion—and as fierce. I'm afraid you'll have to be the one to lower your pride.'

'I wouldn't mind that,' Chryssanti told her. 'But Dimitri will never listen to me—even in the unlikely event of my being alone with him. I know he won't.'

'You'll have to *make* an opportunity to be alone with him,' Lena said firmly, 'and you'll have to *make* him listen. Now,' she looked at her watch, 'it's almost time for dinner. I must go and dress. So must you.'

'Lena,' Chryssanti pleaded, 'I can't face everyone tonight. I certainly haven't got the courage to face Dimitri. I... I'm not very hungry. I'll just go to bed.'

'Facing Dimitri *is* going to take a lot of courage,' Lena agreed. 'But I think you ought to get some practice for when you have to face him alone. Come on, love,' she gave the younger girl a hug, 'freshen up, put on your most stunning outfit, make yourself look as desirable as possible. If Dimitri really loves you, that'll go a long way towards softening his heart.'

If it achieved nothing else, dressing up *was* a morale-booster, Chryssanti had to agree as she surveyed herself in the mirror.

The cocktail-length dress she had chosen to wear shimmered with all the subtle blues of the Greek sea, the colour complementing and enriching the glory of her red-gold hair. The material clung sleekly, the self-lined skirt flaring out to emphasise her small waist, and the cleverly cut neckline revealed only a tantalising glimpse of swelling breasts. Beneath the dress, because it was such a stiflingly hot evening, she wore only bra and pants. Her long, sun-tanned legs needed no adornment. Her elegantly narrow feet she thrust into matching blue strappy sandals.

She could delay no longer and, quitting her room, she made her way along the thickly carpeted corridors to the main assembly-room. The rest of the household was already gathered there and were just pairing off to go into dinner. For a single instant, across the crowded room, her eyes locked with Dimitri's.

'Dimitri, you will take Chryssanti in,' Thalassios decreed.

Oh, no! Chryssanti quailed inwardly as Dimitri, too courteous to oppose his grandfather, came towards her. One look at the granite set of his sculptural profile and she kept her eyes averted.

Being partnered by Dimitri meant also that she must also know the exquisite torture of sitting next to him. As he pulled out her chair for her, inadvertently his hand brushed the bare flesh of her arm. The sensation made her flinch and simultaneously she heard his quick intake of breath.

Polite conversation was expected at the table, but Chryssanti hadn't the nerve to address Dimitri. As the first course was served, she turned to her left-hand neighbour, Manoli.

'How was Paris?' she asked.

'Superb as always. Not that I saw much of it this trip. It was just a flying visit. How much longer do you have with us, Chryssanti?'

That depended so much on the outcome of her confrontation with Dimitri—if she could engineer one.

'I'm not sure. A day or two at the most.'

Manoli turned away to speak to his mother and Chryssanti was left to her own devices.

'So, when you leave here, you will be returning to England?'

She hadn't expected Dimitri to speak to her. But she should have known he would observe the etiquette.

'Yes.' She didn't look at him.

'I see,' was his only comment.

The rest of the meal passed with similar small exchanges. Chryssanti only toyed with her food, and it was a tremendous relief when her grandmother signalled for the ladies to leave the table.

'Have you said anything to Dimitri?' Lena whispered as they adjourned to the salon.

'Oh, yes!' Chryssanti said sarcastically. ' "Pass the salt," "thank you" and "yes, the weather is sultry, isn't it?" '

'You'll *have* to get him on his own.'

'Well, there isn't going to be much opportunity to-night. Look, Lena, I've done as you suggested. I've shown the flag. But I'm not in the mood for any more social chit-chat. I'm going to bed. If anyone asks, you can say I have a headache.'

When Chryssanti woke early next morning, for a moment she couldn't think why she felt such a sense of oppression. It weighed on her like a heavy obstacle resting on her chest.

Then she remembered. Today, somehow, she had to face Dimitri. It might be her last chance. And the outcome wasn't at all certain. Dimitri's motives for asking her to marry him might *not* have been mercenary. But then, he hadn't mentioned love, either.

She needed time to rehearse what she was going to say to him, she decided as she showered and dressed in a skimpy T-shirt and shorts. The informal clothes wouldn't do for the breakfast-table. But it was too early for that. First she intended to take a walk and marshal her thoughts.

Some last-minute impulse as she left her room made her snatch up her bikini.

She had never ventured beyond the villa's cultivated garden and that wilder garden where the ruined temple lay. Today she felt like going further afield, perhaps to the beach on the other side of the island, which she had heard was suitable for swimming.

Though it was so early, the air held a promise of a hot, crackling summer day to come as, to the protracted musical trills of the cicadas, she made her way up a steep path. Away from the villa, the undeveloped part of the island consisted only of a stone-riddled hillside where a few wild goats grazed industriously on anything green and growing.

Skiapelos was not that large an island, and after about twenty minutes Chryssanti emerged suddenly on to the beach, via a grove of twisted, pitted olive trees which grew almost to the edge of the sea.

The beach of perfectly oval white pebbles overlooked a bay of mottled turquoises and peacock-blues, and for a while she was content to sit and watch the sea go through its repertoire of colours.

But as the sun grew hotter she withdrew into the olive trees, changed into her bikini, then waded into the silky embrace of the sea, revelling in its gentle buoyancy.

She still hadn't decided how to approach Dimitri, she mused as she floated on her back, reluctant to leave the cooling water. But she would soon have to make her way back to the villa. She would have to formulate some plan. She stood up, began to wade back towards the beach, then stopped short.

At the spot where she had left her clothes a tall figure was silhouetted against the harsh sunlight. The glare hurt her eyes and his face was in shadow, but she had no doubt who it was.

Her legs were shaking as she picked her way across the pebbles towards him. She essayed a smile which felt more like the rictus of a terrified grimace, and knew that the answering movement of his lips was misleading, that a Greek smiled not only when he was happy but when he was angry as well. Certainly when he spoke there was no friendliness in his tone.

'Do you want sunstroke, coming down here on what is probably going to be the hottest day of the summer?'

'How did you know where I was?' was all she could think of to say.

'One of the servants saw you coming this way, carrying your swimming things and nothing else.' He indicated a canvas bag that lay at his feet. 'There's a drink in there. You had better have some before you become dehydrated.'

As Chryssanti obeyed, she felt with the Trojan high priest, Laocoon, when he'd said, 'I fear the Greeks even when they come bearing gifts.'

'Thank you.' She took a long draught from the flask. 'I don't know why you bothered about me.'

'Neither do I,' was his unpromising retort.

Chryssanti took a deep breath and summoned all her courage.

'But I'm glad you did. Dimitri, I . . . I have to talk to you. Please!' She forced herself to hold his dark-eyed gaze.

Their eye-to-eye encounter went on for so long, in such brooding silence, that she thought he was going to refuse to hear her. But at last he said, 'Very well! But not here. The weather is soon going to deteriorate.'

She bundled her clothes into the bag with the flask and followed him as he turned to stride away up the beach.

'What were you doing right over here, anyway?' he asked as she had almost to run to draw level with him.

'I wanted to say goodbye to the island. And . . . and to think.'

'You will be sorry to leave these islands?' He sounded surprised. They had entered the shadowy darkness of the olive grove once more, and beneath one of its trees he sat down. A gesture indicated that she should do the same.

'Yes, I shall be sorry to go,' Chryssanti wished she dared sit closer to him, but his manner was not inviting. 'I love the islands.' She wished she dared tell him she loved him too. 'Perhaps, after all, it's something to do with my heritage,' she went on. 'But I feel as though they'd been waiting for me all my life.'

'There's more to it than that,' Dimitri said slowly. 'There is attraction in the compactness of an island. I have travelled a lot, and it is difficult to take in the size of the world. But an island can be known intimately—as a man knows the body of the woman he loves.' His voice had grown suddenly husky, and as his eyes met hers Chryssanti felt liquid heat invade her loins. She would never receive a better cue than this.

'That's what I wanted to talk to you about,' she said shakily. 'Love. You . . . you said I didn't know what love is. But I *do*, Dimitri, I *do*.'

'So?' Magnificent shoulders shrugged indifferently. 'What has that to do with me?'

'I love *you*, Dimitri,' she said desperately. 'You said you'd never ask for my love again—and I'm sorry I didn't know that was what you were asking.'

'And what makes you think now that it was?' His tone was still unrelentingly cold, but she thought she detected a change in his breathing.

'I don't know.' She couldn't tell him she had discussed him with Lena. That would offend his male pride. 'I . . . I can only hope so. And I want to apologise for what I said.'

'When you accused me of wanting you only for your uncle's money?' Whatever else he wanted, he certainly meant to extract the last ounce of her abasement.

'Yes,' she said meekly.

He stood up abruptly and turned his back to her. Roughly he tore a twig from one of the olive trees and began to break it into pieces.

'Since we're being honest with each other,' he said tautly, 'I may as well tell you. I have been in love with you for years. Ever since you first came to Skiapelos as an innocent, wide-eyed eighteen-year-old. Only then you had no eyes for me—only for Christos.'

'Oh, Dimitri!' She stood up and would have moved towards him.

'Stay where you are,' he said brusquely. 'You have not heard it all yet. When you came back to Greece and you still seemed to be in love with him, my jealousy knew no bounds. Because of you, I reached the stage where I hated my own brother.'

'I'm sorry!'

'But then it seemed you were learning better, that you had realised he was not worthy of your love. We became friends, you and I, did we not?'

'Yes,' she breathed. 'Oh, yes.'

'We grew closer. You reacted to my presence, to my touch, to my kisses. But still I held back. I wanted to be sure you had learned to love me before I declared myself.'

His pride would never have permitted her to refuse him, she realised. But he was still speaking.

'And then, that night on Helenos, we came even closer. You allowed me to touch you in places that should be only for the man you loved. But still I wasn't sure. I

withdrew from you. I told you wanting was not enough.
I was hoping you would admit it was more than that.'

'How could I?' she demanded, and now she did move
towards him, dared to take hold of his arm and shake
it. 'How could I be the first one to mention it? Do you
think you're the only one with pride? I thought you
meant *you* only wanted *me*. You didn't say anything
about love, either.'

But he wasn't finished yet.

'And then—in Athens—you became mine—totally
mine,' he qualified fiercely. 'You had spoken of returning to England. And I could not let that happen.
And when you let me make love to you I thought you
felt the same.'

'I did! I did!' In weary anguish, Chryssanti rested her
head on his shoulder. If only he would just put his arms
around her, kiss her, all this conflict would be finally
resolved.

'And *then* you said it did not necessarily follow that
you would marry me. I was stunned. But, to make things
worse, you went on to accuse me—*me*—of mercenary
motives.'

'But I've told you—I'm *sorry* about that. Oh, Dimitri,
you must believe me. I *am* sorry. And I do love you.
Please won't you forgive me? Tell me you still love me.'

He did take hold of her now, but only to push her
from him, at arm's length.

'Very well, I will tell you. I love you, Chryssanti.' But,
as she gave a soft little murmur and tried to move towards him, his arms were rigid barriers preventing the
movement. 'I have always loved you, I shall always love
you.' He paused, and if the pause had been intended for
dramatic effect it was very successful. 'But I will never

ask you to marry me. And now shall we return to the villa?'

White-lipped, she stared at him as his arms dropped away. Her mind was in a tumult, and as though the elements echoed her feelings the weather broke with a startling suddenness and a blast of warm scouring wind like that from a baker's oven.

Chryssanti was too lost in her misery to react. To her it seemed part of her punishment as she continued to stare at Dimitri. But his senses were more alert. He took a swift look at the now lowering sky.

'Quickly, we must take cover. There's no time to get back to the villa. It will have to be the cave.'

'Cave?' she looked at him in bewilderment. 'I didn't know there were any caves here. There's one on Helenos.'

'And there is one here. Not as large or as spectacular, but it will do. Hurry!' He grasped her elbow and ran her through the trees, back towards the beach.

As they ran the wind stung their skins, blinded them with dust and bits of leaf. Wind roared its way through the olive leaves, sounding like a giant breaker on the shore. As they emerged into the open Chryssanti saw that the blue sky had been blotted out by bruise-coloured clouds. The hot, fierce wind increased, then came the rain, plummeting from the sky in great bouts. And, by the time they reached the mouth of the cave, thunder stalked the sky.

Chryssanti had never been the nervous type, and she was not afraid of the elements now. More than the storm, she feared the thought of losing Dimitri. If the *meltemi* had not blown up when it had, bringing the storm with it, they would have been on their way back to the villa. The scouring wind had brought with it her reprieve.

'What would you say,' she asked Dimitri above the sounds of the storm, 'if *I* asked *you* to marry *me*?'

In the livid light it was still possible to see his face. And now Chryssanti witnessed the hauteur of which Lena had warned her, the pride of the Black Lions of Skiapelos.

'No Mavroleon has ever had to wait for a woman to propose to him,' he told her.

'Then why won't *you* ask *me*? You love me. You want me. So why?'

'*Theos mou!*' In exasperation he turned upon her. 'How can I? When to you and to the world at large it will seem I am marrying you for your money.'

She almost collapsed with relief. 'Is that the only reason?'

'Is that not sufficient impediment?' he demanded.

'Oh...oh, Dimitri.' Relief made her light-headed, and she began to laugh weakly. But the sound served to increase his wrath.

'Do not dare to laugh at me.' He advanced upon her and grasped her shoulders. But she couldn't stop, though the laughter was not far from tears. 'I will not allow you to laugh at me,' he growled. Then brutally his lips smothered any further sound she might have made.

His kiss was remorseless, savage, punishing, with not a flicker of tenderness. But she accepted it, returned it, gloried in his possession of her mouth. Her hands clasped about his neck, she strained her body close to his, her stinging lips shamelessly parted.

The kiss became deeper, a ruthless probe, but still she did not fight him, and gradually, subtly, she sensed a change as, like a flame, desire rose between them and Dimitri's fingers began slowly, sensually, to explore the warm curves of her body.

She felt him tremble against her and explosive excitement mounted within her.

'Dimitri,' she whispered against his lips. 'Oh, Dimitri, please love me.' Then wished she hadn't spoken when she felt him freeze in her arms.

He tried to pull free of her clinging hands, but she wouldn't let him. She hung on to him, fighting now for what she wanted most in all the world.

'Dimitri, listen to me, please. No one will be able to say you married me for my money. When I marry, the bulk of Uncle Dom's fortune goes to charity.'

'What?' He could not detach her, but he arched his body away from her so that he could look down into her face. 'What did you say?'

She repeated it, and for a moment she misunderstood the look of fury that crossed his handsome features.

'Why the hell did you not tell me that before?' He didn't wait for an answer, which was just as well because she couldn't think of a logical one. 'And why,' suspiciously, 'should you want to get married when it will mean the loss of your wealth?'

'Wealth doesn't mean anything to me. Love does. Grandfather Thalassios called it sentimental claptrap, but I told him I'd rather be loved by a poor fool than desired for mercenary reasons.'

'If you marry me, you may be marrying a fool, but you won't be marrying a poor one. I *am* my father's eldest son, you know. I shall inherit his share of the Mavroleon Corporation some day. Meantime, my salary as a director is no mean one.'

It was a long speech, but the last part of it passed over Chryssanti's head.

'You said if I marry you. Does that mean...?'

'Yes, Chryssanti *mou*!' Oh, the change in his voice! The frost had melted into a wealth of tenderness. 'I think we understand each other at last. What you have told me removes all barriers. Will you still have me?'

'*Will* I?' she cried. 'Just let anyone try and stop me.'

'Not even Grandfather Thalassios?' he teased.

'Him least of all. The old tyrant nearly ruined my life. And I mean to tell him so.'

'By all means. But let us forget him for the moment, hmm?'

They forgot Thalassios Mavroleon. They forgot everything and everyone for a long, long time, as he pulled her close again.

With impatient hands he removed her skimpy bikini, and her throbbing impatience matched his as they sank to the damp, sandy floor of the cave.

His eagerness tempered by tenderness, Dimitri lingeringly caressed the soft mounds of her breasts, the gentle swell of her hips, the flat firmness of her stomach. Then, suddenly fierce, he pulled her tightly against his own naked body, kissing her feverishly.

Their mutual desire became an exquisite, intolerable thing. He entered her and sensation mounted in matching crescendoes until the final climax left them exhausted, senses bemused.

'*S'agapo*, Chryssanti,' Dimitri murmured, 'I love you. It is not only the islands that have waited for you all these years. I too have waited.'

'And do you think,' she teased, secure now in the knowledge of his love, 'that I was worth waiting for?'

With a growl of mock ferocity, he showed her again just how very worthwhile that waiting had been.

Coming Next Month

Available in August wherever paperback books are sold, or through Harlequin Reader Service.

In the U.S.
901 Fuhrmann Blvd.
P.O. Box 1397
Buffalo, N.Y. 14240-1397

In Canada
P.O. Box 603
Fort Erie, Ontario
L2A 5X3

HARLEQUIN
American Romance®

THE LOVES OF A CENTURY...

Join American Romance in a nostalgic look back at the Twentieth Century—at the lives and loves of American men and women from the turn-of-the-century to the dawn of the year 2000.

Journey through the decades from the dance halls of the 1900s to the discos of the seventies ... from Glenn Miller to the Beatles ... from Valentino to Newman ... from corset to miniskirt ... from beau to Significant Other.

Relive the moments ... recapture the memories.

Look now for the CENTURY OF AMERICAN ROMANCE series in Harlequin American Romance. In one of the four American Romance titles appearing each month, for the next twelve months, we'll take you back to a decade of the Twentieth Century, where you'll relive the years and rekindle the romance of days gone by.

Don't miss a day of the CENTURY OF AMERICAN ROMANCE.

A CENTURY OF
AMERICAN ROMANCE
1900's

The women...the men...the passions...
the memories....

CAR-1

Take 4 bestselling love stories FREE

Plus get a FREE surprise gift!

Special Limited-time Offer

Mail to   **Harlequin Reader Service®**

In the U.S.	In Canada
901 Fuhrmann Blvd.	P.O. Box 609
P.O. Box 1867	Fort Erie, Ontario
Buffalo, N.Y. 14269-1867	L2A 5X3

YES! Please send me 4 free Harlequin Presents® novels and my free surprise gift. Then send me 8 brand-new novels every month, which I will receive months before they appear in bookstores. Bill me at the low price of $2.24* each—a savings of 26¢ apiece off cover prices. There are no shipping, handling or other hidden costs. I understand that accepting these books and gifts places me under no obligation ever to buy any books. I can always return a shipment and cancel at any time. Even if I never buy another book from Harlequin, the 4 free books and the surprise gift are mine to keep forever.

* Offer slightly different in Canada—$2.24 per book plus 89¢ per shipment for delivery.
Sales tax applicable in N.Y. and Iowa.   308 BPA U1D3 (CAH)
108 BPA CAP7 (US)

Name _____ (PLEASE PRINT)

Address _____ Apt. No. _____

City _____ State/Prov. _____ Zip/Postal Code _____

This offer is limited to one order per household and not valid to present Harlequin Presents® subscribers. Terms and prices are subject to change.
                                            © 1990 Harlequin Enterprises Limited

CELEBRATE THE SPIRIT OF

1776

with *Freedom Flame* by Caryn Cameron

Available in July 1990

What better way to celebrate the Fourth of July than with bestselling historical author Karen Harper writing as Caryn Cameron? *Freedom Flame* is a suspenseful tale of espionage and passion, set during our country's most exciting time—the American Revolution.

Meet George Washington and Benjamin Franklin, Benedict Arnold and John Andre. And, best of all, meet Meredith Morgan and Darcy Montour, who braved the dangers of British-held Philadelphia to spy for the American cause—and found a consuming passion that would bind them together forever.

Every reader will thrill to this sizzling story of the passionate man and woman who helped make our country free.

Only from Harlequin Historicals!

HH48-1

Harlequin Superromance®

Hamilton
H·O·U·S·E

A powerful restaurant conglomerate that draws the best and brightest to its executive ranks. Now almost eighty years old, Vanessa Hamilton, the founder of Hamilton House, must choose a successor.
Who will it be?

Matt Logan: He's always been the company man, the quintessential team player. But tragedy in his daughter's life and a passionate love affair made him make some hard choices....

Paula Steele: Thoroughly accomplished, with a sharp mind, perfect breeding and looks to die for, Paula thrives on challenges and wants to have it all . . . but is this right for her?

Grady O'Connor: Working for Hamilton House was his salvation after Vietnam. The war had messed him up but good and had killed his storybook marriage. He's been given a second chance—only he doesn't know what the hell he's supposed to do with it....

Harlequin Superromance invites you to enjoy Barbara Kaye's dramatic and emotionally resonant miniseries about mature men and women making life-changing decisions. Don't miss:

- CHOICE OF A LIFETIME—a July 1990 release.
  - CHALLENGE OF A LIFETIME
    —a December 1990 release.
- CHANCE OF A LIFETIME—an April 1991 release.